MOONFLOWER

KACEN CALLENDER

SCHOLASTIC PRESS

New York

Copyright © 2022 by Kacen Callender

All rights reserved. Published by Scholastic Press, an imprint of Scholastic Inc., *Publishers since 1920.* SCHOLASTIC, SCHOLASTIC PRESS, and associated logos are trademarks and/or registered trademarks of Scholastic Inc.

Library of Congress Cataloging-in-Publication Data

Names: Callender, Kacen, author.

Title: Moonflower / by Kacen Callender.

Description: New York : Scholastic Press, an imprint of Scholastic Inc., 2022. | Audience: Ages 8–12. | Audience: Grades 4–6. | Summary: Moon is convinced that they do not belong to this world: that most of the time they are invisible (unless they stay still too long), that they belong to the stars, and want to go back to them—they live entirely in their imagination with an imaginary spirit guide who can appear in any shape and refuses to speak to anyone, lest their words tie them to a world they reject.

Identifiers: LCCN 2021038254 (print) | LCCN 2021038255 (ebook) | ISBN 9781338636598 (hardcover) | ISBN 9781338636604 (paperback) | ISBN 9781338636628 (ebk)

Subjects: LCSH: African American girls—Juvenile fiction. | Identity (Psychology)—Juvenile fiction. | Identity (Philosophical concept)—Juvenile fiction. | Alienation (Social psychology)—Juvenile fiction. | Imagination—Juvenile fiction. | Mothers and daughters—Juvenile fiction. | CYAC: African Americans—Fiction. | Identity—Fiction. | Mental illness—Fiction. | Imagination—Fiction. | Mothers and daughters—Fiction. | LCGFT: Psychological fiction. | Novels.

Classification: LCC PZ7.1.C317 Mo 2022 (print) | LCC PZ7.1.C317 (ebook) | DDC 813.6 [Fic]—dc23

LC record available at https://lccn.loc.gov/2021038254

LC ebook record available at https://lccn.loc.gov/2021038255

10 9 8 7 6 5 4 3 2 1   22 23 24 25 26

Printed in Italy   183

First edition, July 2022

Book design by Elizabeth B. Parisi and Abby Dening

FOR THE YOUNGER ME WHO DIDN'T WANT
TO BE IN THIS WORLD ANYMORE:

I'm so glad you stayed.

FOR ANYONE WHO HAS ALSO WANTED
TO LEAVE THIS WORLD:

I'm so glad you're still here.

THE TREE OF LIFE

There is a tree growing inside me.

Once upon a time, there was a human named Blue. Blue didn't have a home, and she didn't have parents. You might think that everyone has parents, but Blue didn't have parents because she came from the sky. A star drifted down from the dark one night, cradling a baby Blue in its light. Everyone in this world and in your own world as well is made of stars. Blue was made from a star, too. I guess you could say that star was her parent, then, if you really want to.

But the star didn't know how to take care of a wailing human infant, so it carried Blue on the salted breeze and left her in a bed of blooming pink and red and yellow flowers. Each and every star in the night sky has a single wish that they can gift to any child. The child can ask for anything their heart desires, and their wish will come true. The star tied the wish around Blue's neck. It was a glimmer of light that hardened so it looked like a pearl. There are a lot of wishes in this world that people mistake for pearls. There are a few in your own world also—a whole entire wish, gone to waste behind a glass case in a jewelry store.

"There," the star said, satisfied it had done everything it could for the child. "Now when you're old enough to speak, you can tell me what you want, anything at all, and it will be yours."

PAPYRUS

The pyramid is in the center of the city. It's solid gold. Well, I think it might be, anyway. I've never been able to get close enough to have a good look.

I hide in the shadow of an alleyway. Luckily, right now my skin is so transparent that someone has to be looking closely to see me. I must look like a mirage to the beings here. The only thing about me that's as clear as day is the chain. It's like a warm gold thread looped around my ankle, the end dangling before it sinks into the ground, disappearing beneath me like a ray of light. I've tried to get that chain off a thousand times, but nothing works. I can't cut it, can't bite it, can't untie it. The more I try to tug at it, the tighter it gets around my foot.

There's only way to get the chain off, and the answer is in the pyramid. It has to be. They're both the same golden color. That can't just be a coincidence. Wolf says there's no such thing as coincidences, only signs and messages.

Wolf flutters by. He told me that his real name is something I can't pronounce with my human tongue, in a frequency I can't even hear, and the first time I saw him, he was in the form of a wolf, so the nickname stuck. But right now, he's a bright blue butterfly, lazily drifting until he lands on my shoulder. He's the only being that can see me whenever I come here, even when I'm as see-through as a glass of water. My skin is invisible right now, but the longer I'm here, the more my color begins to fade in. I'm starting to see the outline of my gray T-shirt, my brown skin. *You're running out of time, Moon.*

I know.

I slip out from the alley and keep close to the walls of the busy street. All sorts of beings are in this town, ambling around. One rushes by as they pull a rickshaw that kicks up red dust, and another chases after a top hat that's blown away in a wind gust, but everyone else takes their time, looking around in awe and pointing at the sights. There are humans, some from thousands of years ago, dressed in traditional ancient garb like tunics and shawls and loincloths; and there are humans from the future also, wearing white outfits that glow a faint light, who have evolved to be super tall, their heads so big and heavy it's amazing they don't fall.

And there are other beings, too: some with blue skin and wide black eyes, some who grow feathers from their arms, others who have the faces of lions as they stroll around in white robes, backs straight, chins raised, dignified. One of the lion beings with a puffy red mane pauses, sniffing the air, and turns to look right at me, pupils widening in their yellow eyes. I slip behind a stall where beings sit on stools and eat a slimy green cuisine I don't recognize (are those *slugs?*), and a being with pale gray skin and red eyes gasps when I accidentally knock their leg while I crawl past, looking underneath their stool, head turning back and forth as their gaze goes right through me.

Careful, Wolf whispers. *Someone's going to catch you. You're not supposed to be here.*

He likes to find ways to sneak in this reminder. *You're not supposed to be here, Moon.* But I can't let fear stop me now. I'm almost there. This is the closest I've ever gotten to the pyramid. The entire city is like a maze, buildings packed together and stacked on top of each other more and more the nearer I get to the center of the city and the pyramid that waits there. The closer I am to the pyramid, the closer I am to getting rid of my chain and escaping this realm and its world forever.

Wolf flutters around my head. *You should turn back, Moon. You should go home.*

He always says the same thing whenever I try to reach the pyramid, but I shake my head. *That isn't my home.*

The road changes from cobblestone to red dirt to white pavement. The shops and houses are mixtures of cultures and civilizations throughout time. A tall red pagoda looms over a circular mud brick home with a thatched roof. A coffee shop with cushions sits beside a giant coliseum with white pillars. A giant mosque with white towers is surrounded by a canal that grows palm trees along its banks, where riverboats and canoes and ancient red rafts sail by. There are buildings from the future, too. Skyscrapers that go so high I'm pretty sure they're touching the other realms, dazzling with white-blue-silver light. The sky that waits above is a swirling universe of colors, a kaleidoscope of patterns and designs. There's so much waiting in the beyond.

I stop beside a movie theater that looks like it's from the 1950s (it's even in black and white) and peer around the corner. Just a few streets away, I see the tips of the walls. The center of the city's maze has a redbrick fort surrounding the pyramid, and the only gate opens to a drawbridge over the moat carved from the river that snakes through the city's streets. There's a line of what looks like hundreds of people waiting to get inside. No way I can just sneak past all those people and make it into the pyramid. But it looks like the only other option I have is to swim across the moat and climb the huge wall. I feel ripples of frustration. Why does it get more difficult to reach the pyramid every time I come here? It's like a video game that gets harder whenever I lose and try again. Maybe Wolf is right. Maybe I should just give up. He says the pyramid isn't meant for me yet.

I know it seems impossible now, but there's so much waiting for you still. Stay.

Wolf talks like a know-it-all, just because I'm human and just because I'm twelve. He must be hundreds of thousands of years old, but it doesn't matter. He has no idea what my life is like. None at all. He says that he always watches me from afar, even when he isn't by my side, but he doesn't know what it's like to be me. He doesn't feel everything that I feel. He doesn't know how much it hurts when I cry myself to sleep. It's a physical pain, right there in the center of my chest: all the years of the hate built up, hate I've ever received from everyone around and sometimes even from me.

Time is ticking. Time always passes here so much more quickly. A few hours can feel like just a few minutes. My skin is coming in more and more, like someone you might see beneath the waves of the ocean, fading in and out and in again. It won't be long before I look like a solid being, just like everyone else here. And if I look like everyone else, that also means they'll be able to see me. I'll be caught, captured, and who knows what would happen then? I don't want to find out the answer to that one.

I have only a few minutes left. I don't have any choice. I have to make a run for it.

I take a deep breath, get ready to run, and—

It begins.

The scream.

I gasp and spin around. The screech was so loud I thought its maker would be right behind me, but nothing is there. Nothing but other beings, also twisting and turning in surprise.

It's here, Wolf says.

The Shadow. That's what Wolf calls it.

My skin prickles with fear. I lose my breath. The Shadow comes almost every time I'm here. Usually, I have at least an hour, just as I become completely solid and have to return home again, but today, the Shadow has found me early. The monster is like a siren. It seeks out children like me. Screams and alerts anyone nearby that I'm here when I'm not supposed to be. What's scariest is that I've never actually *seen* the Shadow. It's shrouded by a black haze, like smoke gushing into the air. What's waiting for me beneath? It could be anything. It could be a monster, a giant spider with hairy legs and fangs, a wraith reaching for me with dead hands. Wolf has suggested that I don't run. *Stand and face the Shadow. See what will happen.* I think beings like him have a different definition of fear.

My skin is almost completely solid now, and with the Shadow's screams going off, everyone's looking around. Some beings stop in the street and point at me, their eyes wide. Their whispers echo.

Is that a child?

Look at the chain around their foot.

How did they get here?

Is it my imagination? It looks like smoke is gushing over one of the buildings just a street away, the Shadow coming closer.

Moon, listen to me, please, Wolf says. He lands on the tip of my nose. His wings open and close. *You have to go back now. If you stay long enough to become solid . . .*

But I'm too close. This is my last shot. It's the closest I'll ever get to the pyramid. I ignore him, turn around, and run.

Beings gasp and jump out of my way as I rush toward the fort's walls. I run across the street and jump out of the way just as an old-time automobile races by, blaring its horn. I slip past the line of humans that wait, the line curving around the fort's walls, gazes and gasps following. I run onto the drawbridge, feet thumping against the wood, toward the opening. The pyramid is huge so up close, as big as an enormous castle, and there—right there, at the bottom, is an entrance, like a square archway, but it's too dark to see inside—

I blink, and when I open my eyes again, a being

has appeared in front of me. I slide to a stop so fast I almost fall.

The being looks human. She's tall, with pale skin and red-pink hair that matches her dress, which flares around her legs. I know who she is. Wolf has told me all about her, and I've seen her from afar, strolling through the streets with a gaggle of courtiers. She's the Keeper. She oversees the pyramid—this entire city and the lands that surround it.

"Don't you know that it's rude to skip a line?" she says.

I take a step back. There's an echo. A blare. The alarm. I'm yanked *down.*

STAR ANISE

The first thing you should know is that I am not from your world.

Maybe I should have said that first, before anything else, but I know you wouldn't have believed me, and it was better to start somewhere else, so that you could trust that I am a reasonable sort of person who would not make up something like that.

We're all from the other world, actually. It's where we each begin, and where we go when we're asleep, and sometimes even when we're still awake, our eyes open and our minds drifting, until something in the world of the living grabs our attention, alarms beeping and mothers shaking our shoulders, forcing us to come back again. You see, we're much more than just our bodies, and we can do amazing things when we close our eyes. We call this the real world, but it's not any more real than the other side. I guess that means that your world could be imaginary, too, in the end, right?

Maybe I should start again. The first thing you should know is that none of us are from your world, and I'm pretty sure I'm the only living person who knows. I remember being born. I remember the inside of my mom's tummy, her pounding heartbeat and faded laughter muffled by her skin, her gentle hand a shadow against the light that shined through, the moments she cried when she thought no one could see and all those nights she whispered that she already loved me. I remember not being alive. I remember the higher realms, the swirling patterns of colors and the infinite light. I think I might be the only person who remembers, because no one ever talks about the spirit world to me—but maybe it's just that every single person in the world remembers, but none of us ever talk about it out loud, because we're all afraid we'll sound weird or crazy.

LEMON

I open my eyes.

I'm sitting on my bed, legs crossed under me. I've been sitting this way for so long that my feet are asleep. They tingle and sting when I move them. The gold chain is gone.

The sun is rising, yellow light splashing across the sky.

I'm back. I'm in your world again.

Disappointment sinks in.

It takes me a second to breathe and feel settled in my body. It takes a lot of energy to travel to another realm. There's even a word for it. *Astral projection.* I didn't know there was a scientific term. I just figured it was something I could do, if I wanted, and a year ago now, I sat down and closed my eyes and breathed and imagined leaving my body. I went back home—to my real world.

But when I go to the spirit world, the gold chain appears around my foot and never lets me stay long or go very far. There are so many other realms. Wolf told me, once, that it's easiest to think of all the different realms like the layers of a cake, stacked on top of one another. The universe is a giant layered rainbow cake. I've only gotten to the first layer. The pyramid would give me access to the rest of the universe, but I've been trying to get into the pyramid for months now. I always run out of time. It's like the body I leave behind in your world has an internal clock in its brain, and no matter what I do, after exactly one hour, an alarm blares and I'm yanked back down into my body again.

Well, I guess I'll just have to go back and keep trying.

But the Keeper. She saw me this time.

That can't be good, right?

I'm not supposed to be there. I'm a human child who's still alive. The Keeper protects the pyramid and ensures that only people who are allowed to be there go into the stars. She'll probably have patrols watching out for me now, and what about the Shadow? It came even faster than usual this time. It's probably getting better at sniffing me out. It'll find me again, and that scream, that horrible scream, makes me feel like millions of baby spiders are crawling through me.

Wolf told me that the rest of the universe can wait. *You're alive now,* he said once. *You're experiencing the universe, and all its layers, when you sit and look up at the blue sky and feel the breeze against your cheek and feel peace.*

He likes to think he's a poet.

He doesn't have any idea. None. He doesn't know how hard it is, to be alive still, in a world like this one.

But it doesn't matter.

Because I'm going to find a way to get to the pyramid and into the stars.

BLESSED THISTLE

I told my mom that I want to leave your world for mine.

She was so mad that she didn't speak to me for three days.

When she finally spoke to me again, she said, "I've given you a good life, Moon. I don't understand. Why would you want to leave me?"

She knows that it isn't my fault.

It's just the chemicals in your brain.

But she thinks it's selfish of me, to want to leave this world.

She doesn't meet my eye very much anymore.

MAHOGANY

In your world, my bedroom window looks out over a street that used to be filled with people selling perfume and fried bread covered with cinnamon and hats and purses, and records playing music that old people loved to listen to, and that I did, too, depending on my mood, but the street is empty now. It feels like this room, looking out at an abandoned street, is where I'll be trapped forever. This is where I will grow up, and this is where I will watch the world end. That's what it feels like, anyway. (People like to say that I'm too dramatic. Oh, well.)

There isn't very much in my room. Just four empty white walls, a dresser, and a desk that has my journals, which are filled with my stories. That's all I do for days, sometimes. Write and write and write. The window lets in too much sun. It shines even on the hardest days, like the sky is trying to force me to be happy. I like gray days instead: fog drifting through the air and light drizzle tickling my skin. Those are the days when I think it's okay to feel however I want to feel, no matter what anyone else thinks. Adults like to say children can't be sad. "What do you have to be sad about?" They turn to one another and laugh like they're sharing an inside joke. I think this has more to do with adults and how they want to feel instead.

It's summertime. I spend the entire day in my room, writing and staring out my window. But summer is going to end soon. School is going to begin again in just a couple of weeks. I'd rather stay inside by myself. At least here, I'm safe from people who want me to know how much they hate me. At least here, I can always escape into my head.

My mom knocks on the door and walks into my room and sits down beside me on my bed. "How're you feeling, baby?"

She smooths down my hair.

"Are you doing okay today?"

My skin is as dark as my mom's, the kind of skin she says has its own kind of power. Her thick curls are pulled back into a bun, and she has on the light gray nursing outfit she wears when she visits patients in their homes.

"It's such a beautiful day. It would've been nice to spend some time at the park. Remember when we would go out for a walk in the afternoons? Well, more like I would drag you along." She lets out a sound that mimics a laugh, but she isn't really laughing. Why do adults do that so much? Laugh, when something isn't really funny. Smile, when they aren't really happy. "I wish so much was different."

My mom's patients are dying. Her job is to help them feel comfortable so they can transition in peace when they leave this world for mine. I think that's when most of us will realize there's nothing to be scared of, when it's time to die. Her patients close their eyes, and without their bodies, they can rise into the other realms. They're greeted by beings who love them, like Wolf when he first greeted me. My mom is brave. She has to be, to let herself care about people she knows are going to pass away soon, and to raise me all by herself, too.

"I've been thinking, Moon," my mom says. She's always doing some sort of thinking. "Maybe it's time you start talking again."

I don't say a single word, especially to that.

She pushes her glasses up into her curly hair, leaving behind a purplish indent on her nose. "It doesn't help— you know, the way you've been feeling—if you're just cooping up all these thoughts inside."

The way you've been feeling. My mom almost never talks about what I said almost six months ago. This is the first she's mentioned it in weeks. *I don't want to be here anymore.*

"If you explain what's going on inside of your head, maybe you won't be so sad. You'll start to feel better if you'd just speak again."

But most days, nothing's going on inside my head.

Just a numbness prickling over my skin.

An emptiness, and I realize I'm not in my body again.

I don't feel. I can't think.

The doctor diagnosed me with depression. *It's just the chemicals in your brain.*

"It'll help, Moon, if you open up. It'll help both of us."

I decided to stop talking a few months ago now. There's no point in speaking when I can't describe this feeling. It's like a black hole in the middle of my chest. It consumes everything. Light, sound, emotion, thought. The black hole grows, and I don't know how to exist.

Sometimes I forget that I no longer speak, and I answer when my name is called—but most days I won't say a word because I can't hold the weight of life in this language that we humans have made with our hands and our tongues. I think we should create a new language. Words that we can use to describe the feeling when you sit and breathe and grow an entire universe, blossoming and curling and dying in your chest. What is the word for that?

My mom sighs. She kisses my forehead. "I have to go to work. There's dinner on the stove, okay?" She has the midday shift: three in the afternoon to nine at night, every day.

I can hear her out in the living room and kitchen, grabbing her keys before she clicks the apartment door shut behind her, bells jingling. My mom tied Christmas bells around the knob of the apartment door because I have so many dreams that sometimes I sleepwalk right out of my bedroom. My mom was afraid I would sleepwalk out into the city and that she'd never see me again, so she tied on the bells that ring every time I open the door. I think that if she could, she'd tie some bells around me, too—try to figure out when I'm trying to leave this world.

I want to stay in the other world. The world of the living isn't for me.

My mom used to whisper that she loved me, before I was born, but I think she's changed her mind now.

I think she regrets having me.

She didn't know that I would be so sad.

She might love me more if I were a happy child instead.

With every breath, I can feel the black hole in my chest growing, waiting to suck me in so that I'll disappear. I go to the other side every night, but the gold chain always forces me to return—thrown back into this world that you know, lying in bed with my eyes open, wishing that I hadn't woken up again.

EYEBRIGHT

Here's the thing about your world: It's more like a dream the longer you close your eyes. Sometimes I'm not sure any of this is real. Maybe the spirit world isn't real, either. Wolf says that's where imagination comes from—ideas and stories floating through the realms until they drop out of the sky like falling stars and pop into our heads. Have I made up everything in the spirit world? Maybe Wolf is just a character in a story. And what about me? Maybe I'm just a piece of someone else's imagination. Maybe you are, too. Hmmm.

I visit my world late at night. It helps to sit and breathe when most people around me are asleep. If everyone is dreaming, then the reality we've all created falls away and the veil between realms gets thinner. It's three in the morning, and I close my eyes and breathe. And I breathe. And I breathe some more. It feels like hours can pass, sometimes, before I feel the jolt. Wolf says we have multiple bodies, and one of my bodies—the one most people can't see—starts to separate from my physical body, the one I was taught is real. I go *up*.

My physical body still sits in my bed, my legs crossed beneath me, my eyes closed. And I keep going up, until I see my apartment building and my street and the whole city and the country, little dots of yellow lights, and the entire world, until I reach the first layer of the giant rainbow cake. Passing through into the spirit world is like stepping into a fun house with mirrors facing from all sorts of directions, showing a million different reflections—me, over and over again, sitting on my bed and walking with my mom when I was young, holding her hand, and running into the park. And then, like I'm emerging from water, I enter the realm.

I'm outside the city. This is always where I end up first, at the very start of the video game, far outside the maze. The city is several football fields away, shining in the distance. In your world, usually a city is surrounded by neighborhoods with houses, or shops, or *something*, but no—this city just starts exactly where the very first building sits. I can even see the very tip of the golden pyramid.

I'm completely invisible when I look at myself. The only clue that I'm here at all is the gold chain that's looped around my ankle again. I'm standing on solid ground. At least, I think it's solid. Maybe this world changes, depending on the person—becomes something completely different, depending on what we want to see. I'm in a field of grass. Sometimes the ground here is like a mirage. I glance down and see a pool of black space and the blue-and-green globe of Earth far below.

The sky here is made of swirling colors that look like the solar winds in your world, green and blue and yellow shimmers like waves of light, before those lights come together and form a pattern like fireworks in the sky, until the pattern melts away again. Wolf tells me that the lands here are what your world is based on: the rain forests, so full of trees that there isn't enough air to breathe, the oceans with waves as high as mountaintops.

It's like I summoned him with just my thought. He always appears, waiting for me in this realm. It's how I first met him. The first time I left my body, I soared through the air and shot straight up so fast that I flew into this realm and fell onto the ground. Wolf was— well—a *wolf*. He was tall, as tall as an apartment building, with black fur and yellow eyes. He tilted his head as he stared down at me. *Hello, Moon.*

There'd been a lot for him to explain, starting with why a gigantic talking wolf knew my name. *I've always known you. I've always watched over you from this realm,* he said. He's a small mouse today, scurrying through the grass and stopping on my see-through foot. Sometimes I think he chooses smaller forms whenever I'm here. Who knows? Maybe when I'm not in the spirit world, he walks around as a dinosaur.

It's been some time, little Moon, he says. Time moves so much faster here, and the longer I'm away, the more time has passed. Five minutes in your world is ten minutes here. Ten minutes in your world is thirty minutes here. And so on and so forth, until an entire day away from the spirit world means that almost fifty entire years have passed.

I don't speak. I don't have a voice on this side of the veil. But that's all right. He knows my thoughts. He can hear them just fine, as long as I think loud enough.

His voice bounces around in my head. *Are you going to try to get into the pyramid again?*

I bend over and scoop him up, and he sits in the palm of my hand, staring at me with beady eyes, his whiskers twitching. *Not tonight. I have to figure out a new plan first.* Running through the city's maze hasn't worked, and I have to figure out a way to make sure that I'm so fast that no one will catch me. Not the Shadow, not the Keeper, not anyone. There must be a key to the maze of buildings and towers. Maybe there's an underground tunnel that would take me right to the pyramid . . .

In the nights when I don't run through the streets, attempting to make it to the pyramid, I spend time with Wolf in the lands that surround the city. The land behind us goes on and on, maybe for all eternity. I walk, Wolf turning into a hawk that soars over me and then landing on the ground to become a fox that scampers by.

A thought suddenly hits me. Why haven't I ever asked him before? *Wolf, were you ever alive as a human?*

Oh, yes. I've had many lives as a human, he tells me. *I was an emperor once, you know.*

An emperor? Really?

An emperor of Rome. And I was also a boy who lived in a van. I loved to surf. And I wasn't only a human. I was a wave, for a split second. That was one of my favorite lives. The pure joy and thrill for that one moment was wonderful. I have been an astrophysicist and an ant. I was a famous model and I was a rock. I have lived hundreds of thousands of lives, and I could live millions more.

Would you ever want to live again?

Wolf squeaks enthusiastically. *Many of us here in the spirit world dream of the moment we will have the chance to live again. There are so many lives I could experience still.*

But why? I ask him. *Why would anyone want to live? What's the point of being alive?*

I'm excited for the moment you discover the answer to that yourself.

I sigh. Wolf loves to speak in riddles.

I fall into silence while I walk beside him. In our silence, I think about the first night we met. I'd thought I was dreaming. I've had many other strange dreams. I've been on spaceships with aliens who asked which planet I would like to visit next, and I've swum with dolphins while we laughed together under the sea. When I first appeared before Wolf and tried to speak, nothing came out of my mouth. (This was how I got the idea in the first place, you see—to stop speaking on both sides of reality.)

With your head, Wolf had said helpfully. *Think what you mean to say.*

Where am I? I'd asked. I thought it was interesting that when I opened my mouth to speak, no sound came out. I shouted the questions in my head, to make sure he heard me. *What is this place? Who are you?*

Not so loud, Wolf said. *There's no need to shout.* He told me that I was in another realm, and that every human still alive in your world has a group of beings who watch over you. The beings all have different roles. *You often meet us as children. You think that we're your imaginary friends, when you get older.*

Where are the others? I asked him.

They're in the different realms, he said. *You'll meet them, someday, but not now.*

I'd been so curious. *Why was I able to come here?* I asked. *Why not anyone else?*

Wolf has always been patient. He didn't mind that I had so many questions. *It takes a certain type of human.*

I could only think of one sort of human that might be. *Do you have to be sad, like me?*

No, no. You must simply be the sort of human being who likes to be different, who likes to be strange, who likes to question their current reality.

I shook my head. *What do you mean?*

Not all humans want to be different, he said. *So many are quite happy to be the same as everyone else, exactly as they are, and this is just fine, because it's wonderful to be any sort of human being. It's a miracle. An infinite number of lives in this universe, and you get to be human? Incredible, really. But some are not as content to go along with what the majority thinks. They don't believe everything they are told. They like to ask questions, to wonder and ponder about existence and their world.*

This was exactly me. In school, I was always so curious, but whenever I asked a question, my classmates only ever laughed at me. *Why don't humans have tails? Why are we always expected to agree with what the majority believes? Most people thought the world was flat once, didn't they? And that the sun revolved around our world, too. Why is it weird to think we're not the only beings in the universe?* My classmates told me that I was annoying, and they rolled their eyes and sighed loudly whenever I raised my hand.

They didn't want to be different from one another, either. They all went along with the decision that everyone should hate me.

Wolf stared down at me, his yellow eyes glowing like two moons. *The people of your world who prefer to be different from everyone else—well, yes, sometimes they might be unhappy, sensing that there's so much else to your concepts of reality.*

Is that why I'm so sad all the time? There doesn't have to be a reason for depression. That's what the psychiatrist told me and my mom. But for me, even before so many people showed me how much they hated me, I've always felt unhappy. *There has to be more to life than this. Why am I here?*

The swirling lights of color above us come and go. There are pale flowers that grow in the field. Inside each flower, shining through the petals, are glowing seeds. The lights are the size of small marbles, or maybe pearls. The seeds' glow and beat like tiny hearts, fading in and out. I reach my small hand into each flower, and I pluck out the lights. They look like miniature stars in the palms of my hands, but they're ice-cold to the touch. Twelve years ago now, this is what I would have been: a light inside a flower, waiting for my turn to live. Wolf told me once that my seed of life is still inside me, even if I can't see it.

Wolf watches closely. *These lives are very precious, little Moonbeam. Each and every life is precious.*

I nod and cradle the lights in the palms of my hands. Wolf told me once that, eventually, a breeze would come by and take these lives to the end of the plains, but why not help them along? We walk several miles across grass and flowers, petals floating upward like snow drifting back into the sky. A silver river carves through the field and trickles off the edge like a waterfall. There's nothing but black space at the end of the field, a cliff that crumbles into nothingness. I think I might see the glimmer of what looks like glass, and a zillion reflections of your planet facing an infinite number of different directions before they disappear.

A breeze blows before it grows into a wind. I release the orbs of light, and they dance along before they break apart like daffodils, vanishing into the darkness. New lives will begin now. I hope they're happy with theirs. Happier than I've ever been with mine.

Very good, little Moon. Well done.

There've been so many nights when I've hidden beneath my bed's covers as I cried, whispering that I wanted to die. I prayed that if there is a God, I would be taken away in my sleep so that I wouldn't have to live another day. I would be so disappointed whenever I woke up again. I wondered then: What is the point of life? What is the point of being alive, just so I will feel sad all the time?

I hesitate, then ask Wolf, *What if one of these new souls doesn't like being alive? What if they wish someday that they'd never been born, like me?*

Wolf turns into a wolf. I think it might be his favorite form. He's enormous. His paw is as big as me. His fur is warm and comforting. *Do you wish you had never been born, Moon?*

I feel a flinch of shame. Wolf is the only being I can admit this to. When I told my mom, she'd been so angry with me. Disappointed that her child wasn't who she wanted me to be. *Sometimes,* I tell Wolf. But no. That isn't true. *Almost all the time. I can't remember the last time I was happy in that world.*

Wolf huffs a steam of breath, black nostrils flaring. *I know that it hurts now. Please believe me, Moon. It won't hurt forever. There's so much I want to say to help ease your pain, but maybe I should listen to you more instead.*

What's the point? I ask him. *Sometimes it doesn't feel like there's a point to anything.*

I'll tell you a secret, he says. *You chose to be alive.*

What do you mean?

You are the universe. Isn't that true? The roots and branches and leaves and fruits—maybe they think they're separate from one another, too. But they all come together to form one tree. You are the flower of a tree, and since you exist, you are a part of the universe itself. You, the universe, wanted to have a life as a child named Moon. You chose to come here. You decided to live.

Wolf can be so confusing sometimes, and even for the parts that I think I understand, I don't believe him. I shake my head. *Why would I ever decide to be alive, just to be in so much pain?*

Why indeed? Hmmm. He pauses, sniffing the air. *Maybe that's the answer you must seek. The question every human asks, again and again throughout civilization and time. What is the purpose of life itself?*

I wait for him to answer the question, but the sound of a chuckle echoes in my head.

There isn't anything I can say that will answer these

questions for you, Moon. You need to discover the answers for yourself. That's a part of life, too.

I'm still thinking about this even after several minutes pass. Wolf and I stand beside each other silently. There's nothing but the sound of the gentle breeze and my breath. I think about the Shadow. It'd been so quick to find me the last time I was here, but it looks like the monster has decided to take a vacation from hunting me down. Maybe it disappeared, somehow, in the last fifty years. Wouldn't that be great? My skin is becoming more and more solid, and pretty soon, the alarm in my head will bring me back down to your world again.

That's what I'm thinking about, when suddenly Wolf snarls. He whips around. I gasp, afraid that it's the Shadow, that it's found me after all. I turn and feel a second clutch of fear when I see *her* standing in front of us. The pink hair that tumbles over her shoulders has live butterflies twitching their wings as they crawl up and down her strands. Her dress is an even brighter red than I remember. It's like the Keeper appeared out of thin air.

She only smiles at Wolf when he growls. "Oh, quiet, you," she says. She waves her hand around, and he becomes a tiny wolf puppy with a squeak. My body moves on its own as I stand in front of him. I glare up at her. Her smile widens.

"I thought I smelled someone familiar," she says. "Someone who doesn't belong here."

She reaches for me, and before I can blink, she presses a finger on my brow, right between my eyes. For a second, all I see is white.

GUAVA

When I open my eyes, I'm not in the fields. I'm inside a room. It's like a European sitting room from the 1800s, with intricate designs on the floral wallpaper, and sofas with pink cushions. There's a single square window that opens to the city, with its mixture of different builds and eras. I walk closer, shocked that I'm back in the city again. But even more surprising? When I look down, the wall surrounding the window is solid gold.

I'm inside the pyramid.

Someone clears their throat. I spin around. The Keeper stands in front of me.

I forget for a second that I can't speak. I open my mouth, but no sound comes out. I shout my thoughts instead. *Where am I?* I demand. *Where's Wolf?*

"I don't allow dogs in my home," she says. "Don't

worry. He's right outside. He'll be fine without you for a few moments."

Though an eyebrow is raised, she offers a kind smile. It doesn't matter how nice she seems. My throat closes and stones sink inside me. I'm going to get in trouble. I'm not even supposed to be in this realm. But, despite everything, I'm also excited. I'm actually in the pyramid! After so many tries, running through the city to get here, I've finally made it. The pyramid's interior isn't what I thought it would look like, or what I thought would be waiting inside. Is there a special room I have to find that will take this gold chain off my foot and let me leave for the other realms, so that I never have to wake up in your world again?

"Please, sit down," the Keeper says.

I do what she asks, stiffly, hands clamped together in my lap. She sits down opposite me and sips from a cup of tea that hadn't been there a moment ago. She even sticks out her pinky. "Let's start with your name," she says.

I frown at her.

The Keeper tilts her head to the side. "Hello? Are you there? Oh, don't be shy," she says. She raises one hand and points a finger at me, and a golden light glows in the air, floating toward me like a firefly. It floats right into my open mouth, and warmth that feels like a gulp of hot cocoa spreads through my throat and chest.

Words jump out of my mouth. I don't even mean to. I don't want to speak, not really. But I'm listening to myself, the sound of my voice, and I can't stop.

"My name is Moon."

"It's a pleasure to meet you, Moon."

I put a hand to my neck. I'm so surprised that I keep on speaking without really thinking. "What did you do?"

"Oh, nothing much, really. I only gave you a bit of energy."

"Energy?"

"Yes, energy. I believe in your current civilization on earth, you know energy as *magic*. You see, sometimes we block ourselves from speaking, out of fear of what others will think or say. We stop ourselves from being who we truly are, worried that we won't be accepted because we'll be seen as too different. The magic I gave you let you know that you are safe with me. You have absolutely nothing to fear."

Nothing to fear?

I never considered the possibility.

I've always been afraid, I think. Even the act of being born was terrifying. I'd been so safe before I was pushed out into a bright world with loud sounds, no longer surrounded by warmth and love. I was afraid when my father yelled at my mom and when she cried, and I'd never seen her look so alone. I was afraid when I walked down the street, and people stared or whispered because they wanted to decide if I was a boy or a girl. I was afraid at school, when my classmates laughed at me, and I'm afraid, too, when I look at the news and see how many human beings hate people like me.

My mom doesn't like me to look at the news. She thinks I'm too young, but doesn't she remember when she was my age? There isn't any point in hiding from the truth when I see it everywhere. Black people like me, arrested and killed because of the color of their skin. Transgender and nonbinary people, told that we don't exist, and don't deserve the same rights as everyone else. I think adults like to pretend I can't see the truth to make themselves feel better, so they won't have to talk about how hard the world is, about all the pain everyone feels. *"You're just supposed to be a kid right now. You should focus on enjoying life."* But what does that mean? Just because I'm younger than adults, I don't always have to be happy.

Even when I'm sitting alone in my bedroom with nothing but myself and my four walls and my journals, I can't escape my head. *There isn't any point.* That's what I would tell myself, writing down the thoughts that would always find me again. *There isn't any point to living this life of mine if I'm only going to be so sad all the time.* I would write a question, again and again, and I decided I'd try to figure out the answer myself. *What is the point of life?*

Every single life is precious, child. This is what Wolf always needed me to know. *Yours is, too. You're so loved, even if you can't see it yet.*

The Keeper isn't aware of the thoughts filling my head. She crosses her legs. "Now, then. From what I can see, you are a living, breathing human child who has entered this realm before your time. When I check the energetic footprints of every being and soul who has entered the city, I see that you've come here hundreds of times before, about once every fifty years or so. What are you doing here?" she asks me. "What is it that you want?"

My hands are trembling. I clench them together tighter to stop them from shaking. I wish Wolf was here. He would know what to do. He would protect me from whatever is coming next.

The Keeper sighs impatiently. She waves her hand at me again, forcing words to jump out of my mouth.

"I've been trying to reach the pyramid. I wanted to get inside."

"Oh, yes," she says. "I remember. The last time I saw you, you'd skipped the line and were seconds away from sneaking in. Why did you want to come to the pyramid?"

"I want to reach the other realms," I tell her. Does she somehow have the power to force me to speak the truth? Maybe I shouldn't be surprised. Stranger things have happened in this realm. "I want to get rid of this gold chain so that I can stay here as long as I want to, without being pulled back down to my body. I hoped that something inside the pyramid would help."

"Is that so?" She sips her tea, considering me. "And what's so wrong with your world?"

I don't want to tell her the truth this time. I try to clamp my mouth shut for a second, but a jumble of words puffs out my cheeks until they spill out. "I have a hard time being happy," I tell her. "Other people don't treat me like I'm a human being, and I can't escape my own head. I would rather stay here, in the spirit world, instead."

She nods politely. "I see. Well," she says with another bright smile, "you were wrong. The pyramid can't help you get that gold chain from your foot, and it certainly can't keep you here in the spirit world forever. This pyramid is an amplifier of a gate of sorts. A gate to other realms and other worlds."

My excitement builds. "How do I go through the gate?"

The Keeper laughs. Her voice is like a bird's song. "My dear child, I'm not supposed to tell you that. But, perhaps," she says, slowly and thoughtfully, "I might be able to make an exception and help you find answers that you seek. I might even be able to help you get that gold chain off your foot. Would you like that, Moon?"

I'm not sure why I'm so hesitant. There's something about her smile that makes me nervous. But isn't this what I'd wanted all along? "Yes," I tell her. "Yes, please. I would like that very much."

"Well, then, that settles it. I will help you."

I haven't even realized that my skin has become completely solid. The alarm begins to blare in my head. It sounds distant, like an echo coming over a range of mountains.

Just over the noise, I hear the Keeper speak again. "But, little one—before I can help you, I need you to assist me with something first."

I'm curious. I think it's me, this time, who chooses to speak. "Help you? With what?"

The alarm echoes so loudly that I wince. She only smiles. Maybe she knows what will happen before I do. I'm pulled down, down, down again.

It turned out that the star had put Blue in the gardens of a magician, who'd always wanted a child of their own. They were surprised to find Blue! The baby was gurgling and giggling and gnawing on their toes. For three days, the Magician posted signs all around town, like Lost baby found! and Did you lose your baby?—but no one ever came to claim the child.

"Well, then," the mage said as Blue grabbed their finger with a toothless smile, "I guess I have no choice but to keep you here." The Magician tried to sound burdened by the task.

The Magician's town was on the edge of the ocean, so every day, there was the gentle lapping sound of waves against the stone docks. Salt spritzed the air, along with the scent of flowers that tickled Blue's nose. The town had cobblestoned roads, and there were pink and red and yellow and orange houses that climbed the side of the green mountain. There was a market every morning, where people would open their stalls to sell meat pies and mango and guava and cherry jams. (Mango was Blue's favorite.)

Though not everyone was a magician, many people could do magic. Music would flow from shop's walls, which some of the townsfolk would sing along and dance to, dresses spinning and turning all the colors of the rainbow. Children would play on the side of the road, blowing bubbles from their mouths, bubbles that would float up into the air and through the sky and grow bigger and bigger and bigger until they were as big as other planets, drifting through the universe.

Yes, this was a magical and special place for the star to have placed Blue, and the Magician did everything that they could to make Blue as happy as any child could be. There was food that was so sweet Blue's teeth would ache and so spicy that steam would rise from Blue's ears. There was clothing made from the fluff of clouds, and there were toys that would come to life, and there were books, too—books, books, so many books, each telling the endless stories of other worlds, including your own. The Magician even began to teach Blue a little magic.

But night would come, as it always seemed to do. And no matter how happy the Magician wanted to make Blue, nothing ever worked. Blue couldn't help but feel like something *was wrong. Something was missing. Blue would sit at her window and gaze at the night. She clasped the wish that looked like a pearl that still hung around her neck, and she whispered to the star. "Please. Please, take me back to the sky."*

KANNA

School will begin in one week when summer vacation ends. I get a letter from my principal saying that I'll have three other classmates in my pod. There were more students in every class, once upon a time, but then a disease spread, and there were protests in the streets, and then there were no classes at all. My psychiatrist thinks it was because the world changed so quickly that I am depressed, and talked to my mom, as if I wasn't there, about how much the world's changes are affecting mental health. I wish she would've spoken to me instead.

And now, after what everyone calls the Long Hot Summer, the world has changed so quickly that it can be funny to remember the way it used to be and to think about how I lived through a memory that feels like long-ago history. The pods meet in one small room that has a table and chairs and a big screen where our teacher appears from her living room. We're all given tablets to do our work on. My mom shakes her head and says, "We really are living in the future now, I guess."

We students have to take a test before we're assigned to be one another's friends. The adults pretend that isn't why we took a test and that isn't why we've been put into a room together, but we all know it's true. They don't want us to forget how to socialize with other young humans. Maybe they think the world will go back to the way it used to be someday soon.

I wish the adults had looked at my test results and realized that I'm the kind of person who can't make friends. My therapist, Mr. Richmond, says that there are lies we tell ourselves because we're hurting. "Of course you can make friends, Moon," he said once, right before everything changed, in the days when I still spoke with a voice instead of just keeping my thoughts to myself. "You're a human being, too, aren't you?"

I'm in this human form, in this physical body, but some days I wonder if I'm a human after all, or if I'm just a spirit trapped in this world, desperately trying to reach the other realms again. Maybe that's why I feel like I don't belong here.

Just one year ago, before the Long Hot Summer, I was in a school with a class that wasn't separated by pods. Mr. Richmond says we can't heal in the same places that make us hurt, so maybe it's a good thing that I'm in a pod instead of with the same classmates and teachers that decided I deserved to feel alone. Memories aren't real, but they live inside my body anyway. I can feel the ache of them beneath my skin.

What kind of a name is Moon?

You're just being weird for attention.

Moon, please choose grammatically correct pronouns. (Wolf reminded me that our spirits are not defined by the body we are born into, and that before our current civilization, humans naturally understood this across the world and celebrated the uniqueness of bodies that captured multiple, shifting energies that had lived hundreds of thousands of lives before. We were considered sacred, once upon a time.) *I will not refer to you as a "they."*

You're a freak. You know that, right? That's why no one likes you. That's why no one wants to sit with you at lunch. No one invites you to our parties or sleepovers, too. Did you know that? Did you know that we invite everyone in the class but you?

We all try to keep it a secret, but I think you should know that everyone hates you.

Mr. Richmond said that I can make friends even if no one in the class liked me, but I think he only said that because my mom paid him to.

★

Every pod is allowed to have ten people. I have my mom and my three classmates, and she has only one person in her pod at work, since she's a nurse who goes to people's homes to help them be comfortable and keep them company as they die, so I've still got space in my pod for my therapist, who comes to visit me and my mom in our home once a week. My mom says it's a big deal because he usually only has a therapy session on a screen, and I am the only client he will meet in person. I think it's because he wants to observe my body language, on account of the fact that I no longer speak.

Mr. Richmond is really skinny and short, just as short as I am, and he's Black like me, with gray hair and cheeks that sag. He's always got cat hair on his sweater. He reminds me of a cat, too, since he never smiles, and cats don't smile because they can't—they don't have the muscles in their face to let them smile, not the way dogs and humans can. Mr. Richmond never smiles, but I don't know if that's something he has to do. No one has to smile, not if they don't want to.

He comes into the apartment and he and my mom whisper, whisper, whisper at the front door while I sit only about ten feet away in the living room. The apartment is small, but not just because of the size. My mom has a thing for *stuff*. The white walls are covered with paintings she bought at flea markets or found on street corners, and there are wooden shelves that sag under the weight of plants with vines that curl and succulents and miniature cacti. Miniature cacti are succulents, technically—plants that have learned to exist in arid conditions, containing water inside them.

The door opens into the kitchen, with its sticky white tiles and white cabinets, and then there's the living room, with its beige and stained couch and a TV pushed up against the wall. I begged my mom to get the TV once, years ago, back when I still spoke out loud. "How am I supposed to make friends if I don't know what anyone's ever talking about?" So she bought an old boxy TV, the kind they don't even make anymore, and got a hanger to try to pick up some channels. There was a commercial for *Hoarders* once, and my mom laughed and said, "At least I'm not that bad." But I think she might be pretty close.

When my mom and Mr. Richmond are finished speaking, she makes a big show of going into her bedroom to give us privacy, but I know she will be listening closely. I wish the session would just start already. Then it'll be over sooner, and then I can go back to my bedroom and sit and close my eyes for hours and hours. The Keeper's last words still echo in my mind. She wanted my help with something. With *what*? If I help her, then she'll help me figure out a way to stay in the spirit realms—forever.

Mr. Richmond sits down in a chair opposite me. "Hello, Moon."

I nod at him. It's more than I usually do.

"It's good to see you again." He notices the journal I'd been writing in still beside me on the couch. "What do you write in these journals?" he asks me.

I put a protective hand on top of my journal.

"I bet it's something special, whatever you're writing. You're the observant kind. I can tell. You see everything going on around you, so it's hard to ignore the bad stuff, the sad stuff, the stuff that makes you mad, so you have to write all about it instead. Isn't that right?"

I get the feeling that Mr. Richmond is exactly the same way. I wonder if he's got a collection of journals with all his thoughts and feelings, a museum of daydreams.

"Let's talk about your father today."

Even if I was speaking, there'd be nothing much to say. My dad is separated from my mom—they never even married, so there was no need to divorce, and I know he's alive somewhere on this side, but I never see him much. He doesn't bother to call. That's okay. I don't need him anyway.

Mr. Richmond taps his notepad with his pen. "Your mom thought that maybe your relationship with your father is what makes you so sad. Do you think that's true?"

Does there have to be a reason for someone to be sad? Can it be everything and nothing?

He takes in a breath and holds it as he leans forward in that way adults like to do when they're upset but want to hide it from you. "I wondered if you've given any thought to the question I asked at our last session?"

Mr. Richmond had sat in the chair he's sitting in now and said: *Have you considered the way you might be unintentionally harming others by refusing to communicate?*

I'm pretty sure he meant my mom. I think she might've told him to ask me that. The two of them are probably strategizing how they're going to get me to speak again. They want to force words out of me, make me feel bad for my silence so I'll say something, anything. It doesn't matter. I won't let them.

Mr. Richmond clears his throat. When he is unimpressed and displeased, his chin tips to his neck and squeezes his face flat, frown lines growing. He crosses a leg, clipboard of notes in his lap, still tapping that pen.

"Why don't you speak, Moon?" he asks me. He asks me the same question every session. "Your mother tells me that nothing traumatizing has happened to you. She's mentioned that you have seen her fight with your father many years ago, and that you'd had a difficult time at your previous school, but nevertheless, you spoke for an entire eleven years before you stopped." *Nevertheless.* I've always liked Mr. Richmond's choice in words. "I thought we were making progress, before the Long Hot Summer. Is it fear? Are you afraid because of the way everything is changing and keeps changing and seems like it won't stop? Are you angry? I would understand if you were. There's so much injustice in the world." He takes a breath and seems to be speaking more to himself than me now. "Why do we always live through the same cycles? Over and over and over. Maybe we're supposed to learn a lesson, and that's the only way we can escape from the cycles that plague us, our entire civilization. Please, Moon," he says, switching tactics again. "Your mother cares deeply about you. She only wants to know what's wrong. She only wants to help. I can do that. Tell me why you've stopped speaking, and I can help you."

Wolf told me once that there are synchronicities that follow us. Is it just a coincidence that the Keeper said she would help me, too?

Mr. Richmond spends the next thirty minutes sitting in silence, as he usually does—watching me, waiting. At first, there's a tinge of hope in his eyes, and then impatience. By the time the thirty minutes are up, his eyes have become glazed as he stares off into space, and in the silence we share, I get to know him. He doesn't realize he lets me see so much—the twitch of concern in his brow, the scratch of his cheek as he thinks words that I don't hear but can feel. I can feel his sadness. He is so sad, maybe even sadder than me. He has lost someone he loves dearly, Wolf told me once. A child—Mr. Richmond lost a child before I was even born into a body on this earth. There doesn't always have to be a reason for it, this sadness, but Mr. Richmond knows it well.

When the thirty minutes are up, Mr. Richmond pushes himself to his feet, knees cracking. My mom comes out of her bedroom with a wide smile. "How'd it go?" she asks, even though I know for a fact that she was listening to us.

She follows Mr. Richmond to the door and lets him out with a thank-you and a check. I think it's a little silly, that she's paying him to sit in the living room and watch me not talk. Now that Mr. Richmond is gone, my mom lets me see that she is disappointed and upset. She opens kitchen cabinet doors and shuts them loudly, pulling out plates and clanking them onto the counter.

"At your age, you can't see beyond yourself," she says. "You can't see my life. What I might be struggling with."

Can two different things be true at the same time?

"It isn't easy, working and trying to raise you on my own."

Am I allowed to be sad, even if no one else thinks I should be?

"You have no idea how easy your life is. You have so much to be grateful for, and instead . . ."

My mom thinks that gratitude is the answer. If I'm grateful for my food, for my clothes, for my shelter, then I will no longer be depressed.

"I don't know how you expect anything to get better," she says. "If you won't tell me or anyone what's going on, how do you expect us to help?"

I've tried to be grateful. Tried just thinking about how I've been given so much, hoping this would be the cure. I'm tired of this sadness weighing down my body and all the thoughts in my head.

"When I was younger, I didn't know anyone who went to a therapist. If I was ever upset, my mother would just tell me to pray. Thank God and pray."

I don't want to feel like this. I want to be happy, too.

"I've given you a good life," my mom says. "And I know it's not your fault. But sometimes I'm just so tired."

This is something new. My mom has never said this before.

"I'm so tired of this, Moon," she tells me. "I don't know what to do."

She's tired of this. She's tired of me.

My mom has never said these words, but I can feel the truth of them lingering in the air.

She's more than frustrated, more than angry. Those feelings have passed, and now there's just a desert, a woman trapped in endless sand, her child on her shoulders weighing her down. She regrets that she ever had me. She wishes that I was a different child—a human who used pronouns that most people understand, a boy or a girl who doesn't have the name Moon. She would prefer to have a son or a daughter who laughs easily and makes friends with their classmates and does not have a black hole growing in their chest.

My mom does not love me. How can she, if she wishes I were someone else?

I don't want to be in this world anymore. I want to escape the world of the living. When I go back, I'll help the Keeper. I'll do whatever she asks so that I never have to come back to this world again.

SNOWDROP

Wolf waits for me in the field. He's a fawn, skinny legs wobbling. He's trembling. Why does he look so scared?

Moon! I run to him and throw my arms around his neck, kneeling in the dirt. *You're here. I thought that maybe you decided not to come back to this realm anymore. It's been longer than usual. Nearly one hundred years.*

"I wanted to come sooner," I tell him. "I couldn't concentrate, and I had a hard time leaving my body tonight." It was a lot like when I try to fall asleep, tossing and turning and checking the time every few minutes. What is it that the Keeper wants my help with? What if I mess up, and she decides I'm not good enough to let into the other realms?

Wolf stares, black eyes blinking slowly. It takes me a moment to realize why, and when I do, I inhale sharply and put a hand to my mouth. I'm speaking. With my voice. I didn't even think it was possible, before the Keeper—and now . . .

"It was her," I tell him. "The Keeper."

The Keeper is very powerful, Wolf tells me. *What did she say when she captured you?*

I'm surprised. "She didn't capture me, did she?"

One moment, you were in the field beside me, and the next, you'd both disappeared. I was so worried, Moon. I tried to follow your scent, but a barrier wouldn't let me into the pyramid.

I hesitate. "She was . . ." I can't say she was nice. She wasn't *nice*, exactly. "She said that she would tell me how to get my gold chain off so I can travel to the other realms."

Wolf shakes his head. *You didn't agree, did you? I know that your life is hard now, but—*

"That's what you always say. You don't know, Wolf. You have no idea how I feel."

I didn't mean to sound so angry. Wolf looks hurt. His little legs wobble and he plops to the ground.

"I'm sorry," I tell him.

I want to show you something.

Wolf grows until he returns to his favorite form. He

towers over me, black fur glistening in the breeze, and even though I feel a spark of curiosity, I hesitate. "I have to go back to the Keeper. She's waiting for me." What if too much time has passed, and she's changed her mind about helping me stay in the spirit realm?

She likely already knows that you've returned, Wolf says. *She's probably on her way here now. Let me show you this, and you can decide if you truly want the Keeper's help.*

He bows his head and lets me climb his nose until he nuzzles me with his snout, helping me onto his back. I pull on the hairs at the scruff of his neck, each strand of fur longer than I am. He stands tall, and I'm even higher than I would be if I stood on the roof of my apartment's building, two stories above the sidewalk—but I'm not afraid, because I know that Wolf would never let me fall.

Are you ready?

Wolf usually has patience for long walks, but we must have to travel far away now. Air roars past my ears as we rush forward. Within the blink of an eye, the meadows and the city are way behind us, growing smaller with every passing second. We race across desert plains, whale spirits flying high above. We dive into a sea and run beneath the waves, trees growing from the ocean floor, air bubbles rushing past. Wolf sprints across fields and leaps over forests. Every time I blink, we're in an entirely new place.

It feels like only a few minutes have passed when Wolf slows to a stop. *We're here.*

I climb the back of his neck, wobbling as I try to balance, before I get to his head and stand at the crest. He releases a huff of steam. It's snowing. Flakes fall, clumps gathering on my shoulders and in my curls, but the snow isn't cold, and the breeze doesn't make me shiver. Everywhere I look is white snow glowing in the dim, gray light. I wonder why Wolf brought me here—until, finally, I look *up.*

It's almost hard to see, at first, but once I've noticed it, I can't take my eyes away. The sky is swirling with colors as usual, but there's a concentration of light, a ring of blue and white, a glowing orb that looms in the sky like a moon, wavering and shimmering and shining in and out with a pulse. The light, whatever it is, looks more like an echo—like I'm seeing its shine from beneath a sky filled with water.

"What *is* that?" I ask Wolf.

That, he says, *is the light of a dying star. The light will fall like rain, seeds planting themselves in this plain, and new flowers will grow. More lives will begin again. It'll take a while, though. Probably another thousand years or so.*

Wolf explained this to me once. The starlight sinks into the dirt, and all around the star grows another field of flowers, blossoming with seeds made of life. I'm not sure why Wolf has taken me to see this, until I notice it—the tips of leaves that grow out of the snow. The star's glow has been drifting above this field for a while, maybe even since the beginning of time, and these aren't the first seeds that have grown from its light.

Wolf nods his head so that I slide down his snout. He places me onto the snow, so deep I sink into the ground and it rises to my knees. It feels like I'm wading through a warm sea as I step closer and closer to a dead plant. Its white petals are wilted and yellow, and the seeds are still there, but they're empty. They look like marbles of gray-green glass. I can even see inside them. There are millions of tiny holes. Wolf stands tall over me. He never makes any sort of expression, but I can tell that his gaze is grim.

"What happened to the lights?" I ask him. "To the new lives?"

Wolf steps closer, one large paw beside me. He

inspects the dead flowers closely, and I pretend to do so, too, but I'm not sure what I'm supposed to be looking for.

Do you see these holes? Wolf asks. They look like air bubbles trapped in glass. *These are where the seeds of light should be. The lights are missing. Their lives have been stolen.*

I look up at Wolf. "Who would want to steal the lights?"

Wolf looks at me, and I know what he means, what he's trying to tell me—why he wanted to bring me here before I agreed to accept the Keeper's help.

I frown. I know that Wolf doesn't lie. He has no reason to. But something like this? It's hard to believe. Why would the Keeper want to steal lives?

Even if I didn't speak out loud, Wolf can still hear my thoughts. *I have watched the Keeper closely since the moment she captured you. I followed her to this field, and I watched her take the new lives before they had a chance to begin. I believe she has been growing in power by stealing the light of stars for many lifetimes now.*

Wolf walks ahead of me. He's a shadow against the white snow and sky, even blacker in the pale light. His darkness reminds me of all the mysteries of the vast universe. "Power?" I repeat. He sounds like he's describing an evil queen from a fantasy book or something.

Not only power to control others, he says, *though I believe that's something she wants, too. Power, as in energy. I'm not sure what she's doing with the starlight. I don't know what she wants. But that's what makes me worried. Moon, I don't think it would be wise to trust her.*

I frown. I'm so close to getting rid of this gold chain and exploring the other realms. She can't be such a horrible person, can she? She's offered to help me. "But it's like you said. We don't know what she's doing with the starlight," I tell him. "Maybe she's trying to help these lives somehow. Maybe she's gathering them and taking them to the cliff, like us."

No, Moon. She always brings the starlight back to the pyramid. I can't see what she does with the new lives once she's inside.

"There has to be some kind of explanation, right?"

Before Wolf answers, he pauses—gets stiff and still, ears perking up. He sniffs the air. I'm about to ask what's wrong, when I hear it. It comes toward me like an earthquake rumbling closer and closer, over the hills and through the fields. The cries. The mournful, wailing cries. I gasp and spin, heart like thunder. It seems no matter where I am in the spirit world, those screeches eventually find me. I'd hoped that the Shadow had vanished since it didn't chase me the last time I was here, but that was just wishful thinking. What will happen if it finally catches me? Will its monster emerge from the smoky haze, allowing me to see its face for the first time?

Wolf gazes at the horizon. He doesn't seem as worried. He's always told me, hasn't he? He's always suggested that I let the Shadow come to me. Let it catch me so that I can see what's waiting beneath. *Please, do not accept the help of the Keeper,* he tells me. *Please, stay in the world of the living.*

Maybe he's right. Maybe the Keeper can't be trusted. But the thought of going back to your world, of having to wake up again, of not being able to escape this pain and this sadness . . . It's possible, isn't it? Wolf could be wrong about the Keeper. She could just be trying to help.

The Shadow isn't in sight, but it will be eventually, coming closer and closer to me. I have to leave, now, before it catches me.

"Please take me to the pyramid."

Wolf lowers his head as he agrees.

GINGER

The Keeper stands at the entrance of the pyramid. She smiles as I walk closer. The city bustles around me, many beings pausing to point and whisper and stare. I'm half-solid, half-transparent now, and usually I would be doing my best to hide from the beings of this realm, so it feels strange to walk right up to the pyramid and the Keeper, in sight of everyone who would like to see. Wolf is a rabbit now, hopping alongside me. The Keeper looks as radiant as she did when I first saw her. She doesn't seem to mind that she's been waiting for almost one hundred years.

I stop on the opposite end of the drawbridge. I look down at Wolf. "I'm sorry. I have to go. She's waiting."

She won't let me come with you, Wolf says. *She doesn't like me very much, you know.*

I bend over to pick up Wolf and hug him close. "I'll find you when I'm finished. Once the Keeper helps me, we'll be able to travel to all the different realms together."

He doesn't say anything as I put him back down, turn around, and start walking. The Keeper greets me with a glowing smile. "There you are, Moon. I've waited a long time. I was worried you'd changed your mind."

"No," I say quickly. "I haven't changed my mind."

I look over my shoulder at Wolf, who waits beside the drawbridge, pink nose twitching. I want to ask the Keeper what she needs help with. I'm worried that I'll run out of time. I've already been in this world for at least thirty minutes. But the Keeper doesn't notice that I'm antsy. She puts a hand on my shoulder and begins to guide me. "Come," she says. "Let's begin, shall we?"

When I first opened my eyes inside the pyramid, I didn't get to see what the rest of it was like. The entrance is a black square. The Keeper steps through, and I realize the entrance is more like a barrier. It ripples like water as soon as she disappears behind it. I take a deep breath and a big step. The hairs on my arms rise as energy shivers through me, and then—just like that—I'm on the other side.

I don't know what I was expecting to see, but it wasn't this. There's a long, white marble hallway, filled with elevators.

The Keeper smiles down at me. "Allow me to give you a brief tour." She takes me on the first elevator, its doors opening with a ping. There are enough buttons that the entire wall is filled. They go up to number 100,000,000,000,000 . . . the zeros go on and on. I blink. The pyramid is big, but I didn't think it was *that* big. "How is it possible that there are so many floors?" I ask her, unable to keep the surprise out of my voice.

"The pyramid is only an illusion," she says laughingly, as if this is something I should have known. "We have enough floors to house the spirits of the dead that will soon be moving on to other realms."

Now I can't help but stare at the Keeper. I know that Wolf is old, but she must be really, really, *really* old. "How long have you been in the spirit world?"

She laughs. "What a rude question to ask."

The door pings open again, and we step onto a floor—well, I *think* it's a floor, at least. If anything is truly there, then it's only made of glass. There are glass rooms everywhere, too, above and even below me. The see-through walls show zillions of bright stars in a black sky with swirling colorful clouds.

"When a spirit leaves the body that once housed them, they come here to review their life," the Keeper says, gesturing, as we walk down the hall. I see what looks like humans in each of the glass rooms, eyes glazed, watching something I can't see.

"Spirits want to know what it is that they can learn from every life they've lived," the Keeper tells me. "Some spirits decide to be humans. There's an infinite number of lessons to choose from. Some want to learn how to love oneself and others. Some want to learn how to be themselves, no matter what anyone else thinks, and to use their voice for what they believe in. Other spirits wish to better understand themselves and the universe itself. There's a wide variety of experiences to choose from."

Does that mean there's a lesson I wanted to learn, too, before I decided to become a child named Moon? I gape as I stare around. The glass rooms—are they even rooms?—seem to go on forever. Maybe they do.

"After they've reviewed their life and everything they've learned, the spirit waits for others—friends, family, anyone they've known, the group that they usually experience their lives with again and again. When everyone is back together, the spirits often decide whether they will live another life, and which character they will be this time, and what it is they would like to learn. Some spirits stay behind, to help guide from this side. It's all a very complex system," the Keeper says.

We reach the end of the level. Something tells me that this, somehow, is an illusion as well—the door that slides up, letting us back into a white marble hallway again. Maybe it appeared only because the Keeper decided she was ready to move on.

Something occurs to me. "Have I ever been in one of those rooms before?"

"Yes, of course," the Keeper tells me.

It's hard to believe that I would be in a room like that, with other spirits. Maybe my mom would've been there with me, too, and other people in my life who I haven't even met yet. Maybe Wolf would've been there, too. "Why can't I remember any of this, then?"

"Because you're technically still alive." She gives me a smile as her heels clack on the marble tile.

Another elevator door opens. *Ping!*

I hesitate. "Are there any lessons you were meant to learn, too?"

Her smile becomes colder for one instant before it brightens again. "I suppose every spirit is meant to eventually learn something, in the end."

The door opens again, and I gasp. The floor is . . . outside? We walk onto a gravel path that becomes cobblestone, leading to a giant fountain that waits in front of a white manor. The sky above is bright blue, and the path is surrounded by a garden of blooming flowers. The land around the manor spans on and on for miles.

The Keeper's smile is dazzling. "This is my home, Moon."

My mouth falls open. "This is all inside the pyramid?"

"No," the Keeper says slowly. "This is all inside your mind. But, well, isn't that the case for everything?"

The inside of her home reminds me of the room I was in when I first met her. The floors are a shining white marble, and the walls are covered in floral wallpaper. The ceiling is painted like it's the Sistine Chapel, and there are chandeliers glittering with diamonds. A few paintings have colors that swirl, and when we pass a statue of a fairy, I think I hear a whisper. *What're you doing here? You should probably go.*

The Keeper brings me to the same sitting room where I'd met with her before. I'm confused when I look out the window. As we walked to her manor's front door, the outside had been a garden with blue skies, as if we were back in the world of the living—but when I look outside her window, I can see the bustle of the city again, hear the honking cars, and smell the scent of spicy meals. The sky has returned to the swirling greens and yellows and purples of the spirit world.

The Keeper notices my confusion. "If I open the door and would like to take a stroll through my garden, then that's what will appear before me. If I open my door to take a walk through this city, then that's what will come to me, too. I can go anywhere within this realm."

Wolf told me that she's powerful, and I'm starting to believe it. But if she's so powerful, what could the Keeper possibly need my help with? There's also a nagging feeling inside. I decided to ignore Wolf, but what if he was right? What if the Keeper has been dangerous all this time?

She notices my hesitation with a growing smile. "Darling child," the Keeper says, "you don't have to be afraid of me. I only need your assistance with a simple task."

My skin is coming in clearer and clearer now. I'm almost completely solid. I probably have only a few minutes left before the gold chain around my foot will yank me down. The Keeper is going to need to tell me what she wants me to do fast.

There are plush couches with comfortable silky and satin cushions and pillows, and even though it isn't cold, there's a fireplace with warm embers. The Keeper invites me to sit down and asks me if I would like any tea. I say yes, please, even though the last time I had tea was about two years ago, when I decided I wanted to be more grown up but then decided I really didn't like the bitter taste very much.

"This is peppermint with lavender and honey," the Keeper says, and before my very eyes, a fragile-looking porcelain teacup appears in her hand. She gives it to me, which I take with shaking fingers, afraid to spill a drop.

I try to pretend I am unimpressed and unbothered by her magic tricks as I take a long sip of tea, which sends warmth over my skin.

I put the teacup down on the table and gather the courage to ask, "Are you a witch?"

"I prefer the term *magician*."

"How many magicians are there in the spirit world?"

She gives a gentle laugh. "Coincidentally, the same number of beings that exist in the entire universe. You could be a magician, too, if you really wanted to be one. We're all the magicians of our own realities. You did know that, didn't you? We can get what we want in this universe, whenever we want, because we *are* the universe."

"Really? How do I do that?"

"Finish your tea, dear, before it gets cold."

I'd written about a magician in my journals also. Wolf always told me that we receive our creativity from the spirits. *Spirits are the ones who give you your ideas,* he said. *They write stories through you, to share their messages.* Maybe the very first person to ever write about magic got the idea from the spirit world. Maybe the spirit realm wanted us to remember that we really do have magic, too.

Is it just my imagination? It feels like the chain around my ankle is starting to tighten. "I don't have a lot of time left."

"On to business, then." She puts her teacup on a small porcelain plate with a clink. "I need your help with a little excursion. I'm not allowed to leave this realm," she explains. "I'm the Keeper, after all. And other beings here—well, they wouldn't understand why I need their help with this particular task. You're the only person I can trust, Moon."

I frown with confusion, and I watch as the Keeper stands and strolls to the window. Her back is to me when she speaks. "Moon, I need you to visit a friend of mine. This friend is in another realm, far above this one. I will allow you through the gate using the pyramid, just this once—and if you're successful, once you return, I will take your annoying little gold chain off."

That's what I've wanted all along. Why am I hesitating now? I could finally leave your world forever and stay here, in the spirit realm. Wolf has told me to wait. *Wait and hold on.* There's so much of life that I haven't experienced yet. So many people I haven't met, people who will love me. So many sights I haven't seen and so many stories I haven't written. I haven't experienced the magic of the living.

"Who is your friend?" I ask.

She turns, sipping her tea. "My friend is a magnificent being. It'll be an honor, truly, to meet them." Her smile lightens. "They're a star. All I need from you, little one," she says, "is to borrow some of this star's light."

My breath gets stuck for a second. Wolf was right. She really is stealing starlight. "Why would you need a star's light?" I ask her, but I don't think she likes being questioned.

The Keeper slowly lowers the teacup from her lips. "Why? Well, if you must know," she says, "I need starlight to survive."

"But aren't you stealing new lives?" I ask her.

There's a cold flash in her eyes, but it disappears with a smile. "Oh, no," she tells me. "No, no. Is that what your friend, the little dog, said? New lives will always begin as they're meant to, and I don't take *all* the starlight. Only a little, so that I can go on existing, too. It's better for everyone, in the end," she says. "This city needs its Keeper. I overlook all here, and without me, many spirits would be lost in this realm. You're helping so many by helping me, when you think about it."

I hesitate. I'm not sure what is right and what is wrong. Maybe Wolf was mistaken. The Keeper is taking the starlight from fields, but if she's telling the truth, then it's for the best of everyone—not just for her own power.

"And if I borrow some of the star's light," I say slowly, "you will take off this chain?"

"Yes, yes," the Keeper says, waving around a hand. "That was the agreement."

I stare at my foot. I look completely solid now, with just a few atoms and molecules left. "I accept."

Her smile slowly curls across her face. "Very well, then."

SNAPDRAGON

Summer vacation ends. I have to return to my pod for school again. My mom doesn't talk to me much anymore, but before I leave the apartment, she gives me a big hug, longer than she normally would. She kisses my forehead. "Have a good time," she says. I look down at my feet. My mom almost puts her hand on my cheek. It hovers there, like she's trying to transfer some of her happiness into me.

Gray clouds threaten a thunderstorm, and a heat lingers and swells over the city, steam rising and making everything feel gross and sweaty and wet. I guess that's why it's called a heat *wave*. My mom's apartment was a whole lot cooler, with the AC unit rumbling and spitting frost from the window. It's so hot that sweat flows out from all my pores, and my sweater sticks to my skin.

The city is different from the one I used to know. The

sidewalks are empty. Maybe the world already ended and I just didn't know. I'm scared to be outside, just a little. It's the first time I've left the apartment in months. My mom told me once that she thinks I'm the bravest kid she knows. "Just walking down the street can be an act of bravery sometimes." She meant because of my brown skin, because of the oversized sweaters I wear even in the middle of summer. I always get a bunch of stares, and the same question follows me everywhere. *Is that a boy or a girl? Is that a girl or a boy?*

There's a park I used to walk through, before the summer when everything changed. I step onto the grass, and in that single second, time stops. The cloudy gray sky fades away into a bright blue. Yellow light wraps around me, and puffy white seeds float through the air. Trees are so tall they brush the bottom of the sky.

There's a rustle and a crunch.

I spin around. Someone is there.

They look like they're eleven or twelve or maybe even thirteen, and they have light brown skin and curly black hair, so dark it's almost blue, and big brown eyes. They're wearing a white dress of lace that glitters and sweeps to the ground, the ends tattered and stained. They're barefoot, but their feet don't have nicks and cuts from running around without shoes. But the thing that makes me stare are the scales. Blue and silver scales, like they'd belong to a fish, grow out of their arms and cheeks and neck. The scales are moving and glistening, opening and closing with every breath. They remind me of the sort of being that should be in the spirit world instead.

I must be dreaming, right?

This has to be in my head.

The being looks over their shoulder and it feels like they're looking right through me, like I'm just a ghost that they can't see. They turn and run.

"Hey—wait!"

Those are the first words I've spoken in your world for months, but my voice comes out so strong that it echoes. The echo fades, swallowed by the cicadas' wings. I don't even know why I asked them to stop running. It's not like I would know what to say. And by the time I've walked out of the park, the sky turning gray, I'm not sure they were real anyway.

CHAMOMILE

The classrooms are in little white boxlike pods, spread out across the field of the old school, where people used to play sports and watch from the bleachers. The old brick school building is still there, too, black mold and vines crawling up the walls, the remnant of a long-ago memory. The pods are all far enough away that no one has to get too close to one another, and there are adults lined up, holding clipboards and wearing masks, calling out instructions to stay at least nine feet apart as we go to our assigned rooms. Sometimes I wonder if there are alternate worlds, alternate universes, where there was never a disease at all, and nothing ever changed at all, and there's a different version of me, too—a Moon that is actually happy.

I'm in pod classroom #306. I open the door to find two of my new classmates already inside. They don't

wear their masks, so I take mine off also. I look anywhere but at them. Memories aren't real, but they're just
as alive as you and me. If I close my eyes and think about
the past, then the memory plays like a movie, and I'm
transported back in time. I still have the same emotions.
Laughter echoes beneath my skin. A boy in my class hits
me across the cheek. *Everyone hates you, Moon. You know
that, don't you?*

When I walk in, my new classmates look up at me,
conversation stopped. One is white with a lot of freckles
and pale, curly red hair and glasses that are so thick
their eyes look magnified. The other has dark brown
skin and straight black hair and brown eyes with a lot
of long eyelashes. I know that both of their eyes are
doing more than just looking. They're watching me the
way robots might, analyzing me and picking me apart.
They're trying to figure out whether I'm the kind of
person they will like or dislike. If I'm the kind of person
who can be their friend or not. I've had enough experience with this sort of thing to already know the answer
to that one.

I wish I was in an alternate universe right now. A
universe where people liked it when other people are

different from them. It would be a good thing, in this alternate universe, that people were really weird, or that they had too many ideas that were new, too many thoughts that were puzzling and confusing, too many questions that asked others to think in a different way.

My classmates watch as I duck my head and shut the door. I wish they would look away already. The pod is too small to escape them, and there's only one table, set up with four chairs. I pull out one of the chairs, scraping it as far away from the table as I can, and sit down. I pull out my journal from my backpack. It feels like armor. At least with my stories, I know I'm safe. I begin writing so I won't have to look at them. In this alternate universe, we wouldn't be afraid of what we don't understand. We wouldn't say that our way of living is the only right way. We would all be excited to sit down and exchange all these new thoughts, new ideas, new questions, and come up with a new world together.

But maybe I'm being hypocritical. I'm scared, too. I think about what the Keeper said. We're all magicians. I think our world could really change. If we stopped being so scared, we could learn to be excited by how infinitely different we all are instead. I don't know. When I still spoke aloud, months ago now, my mom used to say I sounded like a fifty-year-old, even though I'm only twelve. Maybe it's because I've lived thousands of other lives. Maybe it's because I'm sad and stuck in my head.

The white one says, "I'm Lilah. My pronouns are she and her and hers. This is Wiley."

Wiley speaks. "My pronouns are he and him and his."

And they both look at me expectantly. Even if I did speak, I wouldn't want to tell Lilah or Wiley my name. People usually like to say how weird it is to be named after the moon or ask why my mom would ever call me something like that. I chose the name for myself. One day my mom dragged me out on one of our walks, way before the Long Hot Summer began, and I told her about the fact that I don't feel like I'm either a boy or a girl. She said that it's beautiful, to be genderless like me. And even though the sun was shining, I looked up and I saw the moon. It was just a shadow, half of a white ghost hanging in the sky, but I thought it was funny that the moon had the power to exist both during the daytime and at night, like it was caught in between different worlds, just like me. My mom asked me if I'd like to change my name, and that's what I told her.

"Moon," she said. "Sounds nice."

Lilah and Wiley are watching me with raised eyebrows, and I realize that I zoned out, and they're both waiting for me to say or do something. Whenever this happened in my old school and my old pod, everyone would start to laugh.

"What, are you shy or something?" Wiley says.

At my old school, there was a boy whose name I will not say because my mom once told me that names have power, and I don't want to give him that. But he would follow me around sometimes. I'd try to pretend I couldn't hear him. I'd put in my headphones, but he'd just shout over the music. Everyone laughed with him.

"It's okay if you're shy."

He'd walk right beside me, so close the teachers in the hall would think we were friends. *Everyone in our class hates you,* he said. *Everyone thinks you're annoying and weird. No one likes you. No one wants to be your friend. No one thinks you should even be alive. Did you hear me?* he said.

My mom hadn't really listened to me when I told her

about the boy and everyone else in my class. *Don't worry about them,* she said. "Sometimes people are afraid when they see someone so powerful they don't understand. If you saw a god or an angel appear from the sky, you would be afraid of them, too, wouldn't you?"

But I'm not a god or an angel. I'm a human being.

My eyes are stinging. I can feel the bewildered stares of Lilah and Wiley as I begin to cry. Lilah goes to call the teacher. "What's wrong?" the teacher asks over the speaker. "Are you feeling sick?" And when I nod, tears squeezing down my face, she says it's okay for me to go home early today.

CINNAMON

The Keeper waits for me in the fields, a wind blooming around her. Even though I'm invisible, her eyes land right on me the moment I appear. "There you are," she says. "I was worried that you'd changed your mind."

The midnight-blue grass rustles around me and the lights above tumble and turn. I look up and down and all around, waiting for Wolf to appear beside me. My heart hurts when he doesn't. Wolf has been here for me every single time I've come to this realm, from the very first moment I took a step here. Maybe he decided he doesn't want to be my friend anymore since I've agreed to help the Keeper. That isn't very fair of him, is it? He doesn't know what the Keeper does with the starlight when she collects it.

There isn't any time for tea today when we get to the

pyramid. The Keeper walks me down a maze of white and gray halls, speaking rapidly.

"Now, remember," she says. "I will extend your time here in the spirit world. That annoying little gold chain of yours means that you don't have free reign just yet, but I can give a temporary extension. You might not want to stay here for *too* long," she says, but doesn't offer an explanation.

Wolf had warned me not to stay too long in the spirit realm. If I stay here so long that I become completely solid . . . Well, he never actually said what would happen, but it probably isn't very good. But I try to push aside any thought of Wolf. I'll finally be able to see what waits in the other realms. I'll finally be free. This is all I've ever wanted, right?

Then why don't I feel more excited? I'm not as happy as I thought I would be. I always imagined that Wolf would be there to see and celebrate my freedom from the gold thread. I want him to be here to celebrate with me.

The Keeper's voice is filled with more excitement than I feel. "I have been trapped here for many lifetimes," she tells me. "I've been unable to leave. But you—you can go anywhere you want to go."

A door slides up, and we step into a room that's pure black—so black that there isn't any light when the door slides shut behind us. My heart beats nervously. It's so dark that I can't see anything, not even my own hand when I hold it up to my face. I feel like I've stepped out of existence and into nonexistence, and that I'll begin to unravel any minute.

The Keeper's voice echoes.

"This is the gate," she tells me.

I turn my head back and forth, even though I still can't see anything. Is something about to appear out of nothing? I thought maybe the gate would be an actual gate, or some sort of machine that would teleport me, like in a sci-fi story.

My voice quivers when I speak. "How does the gate work?"

"Let me show you."

I jump when I feel an icy touch on my forehead, in between my brows. I realize it's just the Keeper's finger, but this doesn't do anything to calm me down. My nerves jump. She doesn't seem to notice.

"The gate is inside your mind," she says. "It's inside

each and every single one of us. Light creates illusions. This room doesn't allow light in, amplifying your own power to travel—anywhere you would like to, across the universe."

My heart speeds up at the thought. "Anywhere?"

"Anywhere at all. You haven't been allowed to leave this realm because you still live, but as the Keeper, I have the ability to give you permission."

Her touch is cold, but my skin tingles with warmth, starting between my brows and spreading over the top of my head. It feels like weights were lifted from my shoulders, and I feel like I'm rising, even when I'm standing still. It's a similar sensation to when I'm sitting in my bedroom, eyes closed, and I leave my body. I can feel it. I can feel how free I am now—free to go wherever I want to go. I'm so close. I'll borrow some of the starlight, and when I give it to the Keeper, she'll take my gold chain from my ankle so I can stay here forever.

"When you visit the star, all you need to do is scoop some of its light into your hands. You're not in your physical body. The star can't hurt you."

I nod, even though the Keeper can't see me.

"Now," she says slowly. "I want you to imagine a

star. Any star will do. Can you do that, Moon?"

I hesitate. Any star in the universe? I close my eyes, even though the room is already darker than night, and imagine the image of a star I'd seen once. A silver-blue-white star, so big that the sun of your world can fit inside billions of times. It's so big that my mind can't even understand its size, not really. Surely a star like that would be willing to let go of a handful of its light. "Yes. I'm imagining it now."

"Good." The Keeper's voice trails, and it sounds like a recording that's been made to slow down, getting farther and farther away. "Very . . . good . . ."

"What's supposed to happen next?"

Silence. The Keeper doesn't answer me. White patterns shine through my eyelids, like light reflecting on the surface of a pond, so I open them.

I thought I was ready to meet a star, but I was wrong.

I had no idea what it would be like to actually stand in front of one.

The star is exactly like I'd imagined. It's made of silvery white-blue light, bursts of energy and streams of beams snaking in and out over its surface, and its surface—it goes on and on, in every direction that I look, side to side and up and down. It isn't like being on Earth, where there's also a sky. The only thing in front of me, for what feels like forever, is this star. It's so big that it doesn't feel possible that something like this can even be hidden away in the universe, which makes me start to feel how big the universe really is, something that my mind can't even comprehend. This must be how a grain of sand feels, floating around in the ocean. No—a million oceans. No. Infinite.

Child.

A being is in front of me. They don't have any features. They're more like a silhouette of light, a mirage that wavers, growing brighter the more I look at them. The being's voice echoes in my head. *You shouldn't have come here.*

I'm breathless. "Who are you?" I ask, voice shaking. I'm still mostly invisible. "How can you see me?"

The Keeper didn't warn me that someone might be here, waiting. It's almost like this being is *guarding* the star. And that's another thing: The star is still behind them, but it's shrinking. It's as big as a skyscraper now, and I still have to strain my head to look *up*, and even then I can't see the top, but I don't feel like I'm disappearing into nothingness anymore.

The being hasn't answered either of my questions, so I ask another. "How did the star get smaller?"

They flicker and disappear before they shine right beside me, just a few breaths away. *Perhaps it didn't get smaller. Perhaps you expanded.*

I gulp. "Are you guarding the star?"

The light tilts their head to the side. *I am the star. You are the star, too.*

They're starting to sound a little like Wolf, saying things that are so confusing. What does that mean? How can we both be the star?

"I'm here to borrow some of the star's light," I tell the being. Well, maybe *borrow* isn't exactly the right word, but it sounds better than saying I'm here to take it.

I'm worried that the being will want to fight, or that it'll ask me questions and I can only take the light if I get the answers right, but they only vanish again. Their voice echoes behind me, and I spin around.

You would be making a mistake, they say. *The woman cannot be trusted.*

The woman. "Do you mean the Keeper?"

She's in such immense pain. She's still running away. You are, too, little Moon.

"How did you know my name?"

I am you.

I wish this being would make more sense. But maybe I need to stop being afraid of what's different, too. Maybe I also need to open my mind to other possibilities. "What do you mean?"

We are of the same energy that composes this universe. Our separation is only an illusion. I know you, Moon. I know all humans, all their fears and desires and wishes. I am all humans, too, as well as the infinite number of beings in this universe.

"If we're the same, then why does it feel like we're separate?"

We began as one, with no illusion of separation, a spark of creation that is still inside each of us, which connects us all. We wanted to experience. We wanted to expand, to grow. Our thought has created worlds, galaxies, this universe. We have created moons, too, and all their phases. Their cycles and changes. And we wait patiently for each of you to return, to bring us what you have experienced and learned.

Everything I've learned. Is that the point of life? To experience and grow? Maybe the purpose of life is this and even more that I can't understand. I ask the star. "What is the point of life?"

The purpose of life is to reconnect with what you have lost. The purpose is to find your way back to your soul's original path on your earth, which brings you such peace and joy. Do you remember what your path is, Moon? When you are young, you remember why you came to your earth, and you speak of your path with passion, until you grow older, and people tell you that this path is impossible, or wrong, or not good enough, and you give up, or forget, or decide that you were only a child, dreaming of the impossible. Do you remember? the star asks.

I think I do. I remember being inside my mother's stomach. I remember feeling loved. I'd felt so safe. I pause, frowning. Maybe my path is to find my way away from fear—to find freedom from what other people say and think. I feel myself lighten at the thought. If I wasn't afraid—if I could be free in my body, free to be myself—then maybe I wouldn't feel so trapped anymore.

"I think it's to not be afraid," I say. "To be myself, even when other people think I'm weird, or when I'm scared."

Perhaps, the star says. *Perhaps it's this and more. There are always cycles. Levels to continue uncovering, discovering, with every lesson you learn, multiple lessons for you all.*

"But that can't be every single person's purpose on Earth."

No, it's not. There are as many individualized purposes on your planet as there are human beings, specific lives and their stories crafted just for all of you to experience what you must in order to learn; then you shed your skin and return, and think about what lessons must be learned in your next life in order to expand again.

And now, the star tells me, *there is another question you want to ask.*

Even if they don't have any eyes, I can feel their stare. "What did you mean when you said that I'm running away?"

Do you think there's shame in this? So many of us are afraid to face ourselves.

More puzzles and riddles, and I'm running out of time. Even if this being isn't the star's guardian, I still feel like I need their permission. "Why can't the Keeper be trusted?"

When they disappear again, they don't reappear—at least, not in a place I can see. Maybe they've gone into the star, its light towering over me. Their voice still echoes as if they're right beside me. *There are some things you can only learn through experience.*

This sounds like the permission I need. I walk closer to the star slowly. Bands of light dive in and out of the star's surface. I reach out a hand to one of the streams. The starlight is cold. It pools in my hands like white water, glittering and glowing. I cradle it in my palms, afraid to spill a single drop. I wonder what it would taste like, but something tells me that I shouldn't drink this starlight, no matter what.

The voice echoes. *There will be three. You'll need their help.*

"Three?"

The first will be waiting. Ask for them when you don't know what else to do.

"What do you mean?"

The answer you need is inside you. You only have to listen for them. They will call your name when the time comes.

"Listen to what? To who?"

But the being—the star, I really think that being might've been the star after all—doesn't answer me. The star begins to grow, or maybe I'm shrinking. It's becoming so big that its original form is overwhelming again, so I shut my eyes. And I breathe.

COCONUT

When I appear in the Keeper's home, the starlight is still cupped in my hands. It's incredible, so incredible it feels impossible, to teleport across realms and dimensions with a single thought alone. It's still draining, though. I feel like I've run a whole marathon, even if I'm not in my body—and I'll have to run some more.

I'm completely solid, my gold chain twinkling against my skin. I've spent way more time in the realms than I ever have before. Wolf wouldn't be happy to know I'm completely solid, fully visible, but maybe after the Keeper helps me, it won't matter.

I've never been in this part of the manor before. The hallways are still and empty and dark, shadows following me, flickering in the corner of my eye. There are so many hallways, so many doors, and any window I see has the drapes tied shut. With every step I take, I just get more and more lost. My hands are cupped together, starlight threatening to spill to the floor. I don't know the Keeper's name—I don't even know if she *has* one—so I just call her the only way I can, again and again. "Keeper? Keeper!"

I pause when I see another door cracked open, a sliver of silver light falling from it. I walk to the door and push it open with my foot, my gold thread dangling.

The room is smaller than my bedroom back in your world, and it's lined with shelves. The shelves hold jars of light—hundreds and thousands and maybe even millions of tiny lights, all the size of marbles or pearls. These are just like the lights that I've helped pull from flowers with Wolf, releasing them over the sea.

A hand grabs my shoulder. I gasp and spin around, almost spilling the starlight. My heart stampedes in my chest. The Keeper's smile glitters. "There you are."

Her hand claws into my shoulder sharply. I wince as she tugs me away from the room, snapping the door shut. She doesn't seem angry. She only stares hungrily at the starlight pooled in my hands.

"Here," she says, cupping her hands together beneath mine. "Give it here."

My heart hasn't slowed down. I'm pulled in two different directions. I want to give her the starlight so she can get this chain off my ankle, but now, I can hear only the star's voice and Wolf's words. *She can't be trusted.*

"Why do you have so many of the seeds?" I ask her. "You said the seeds were to help you stay alive, and that the extras would go on to be lives, but this . . ." It's like she's imprisoned the souls of new lives here, stopped them from going into different realms.

The Keeper doesn't answer me. She slowly lowers her hands, her gaze growing with anger that I can feel, pulsing through the air and growing bigger and hotter with every second. I back away, still holding the starlight in my hands.

"Don't be a bad child, Moon," the Keeper says slowly, straightening. Is it just my imagination that she seems to grow taller? "I've been very generous to you. I'm the only person who is willing to help you."

Is that true? Wolf has always been there for me, even in the moments when I don't want to hear what he has to say. I look around, hoping he will appear like he usually does whenever I think of him, but he still doesn't come. He must be really, really angry with me—or maybe he isn't angry at all. Maybe something is wrong.

The Keeper continues to follow me as I back away. Her eyes are glued to the starlight in my hands. "I have such resentment in my heart, Moon, I will admit to that. I have not received the love, the acceptance, that I deserve. I've been trapped in this form and this realm for an eternity, powerless. I don't understand," she says, "why I haven't been allowed to go to the higher realms."

The Keeper's face is in shadow as she walks. She's scaring me, but she doesn't seem to notice—or maybe she just doesn't care. "I remember my life before this one," she tells me. "Before we all separated into these forms. I remember the peace I felt, and the power. How do I return to that power? I've never figured it out."

That reminds me of my life, too. I remember the peace I'd had, the love I felt for myself, before the world began to lie to me. Before the world started to say that I'm not worth the love I have for myself. The world became too painful, and I started to think that maybe I would never feel happiness again. Maybe the Keeper and I are even more similar than I'd known.

"Oh, Moon," she says, "there was so much power. So

much more than I have now. Just a sip of this starlight will help me feel that power again."

"But I thought you needed the starlight to live."

"I do," she says. Her eyes meet mine. "I need it to live to my greatest potential. The seeds are nothing," she says. "They barely help. But pure starlight—yes, that's what I need." Her smile drops, and the sudden viciousness of her scowl makes my heart stop. There's more rage than I've ever seen on a person's face. "Give me the starlight."

The Keeper had said she would help me, but there's no way I can give it to her now. Wolf was right, and so was the star. I don't know what will happen if the Keeper drinks this starlight, but I know it won't be good. I open my palms to spill the starlight all over the floor—but before it splashes to the ground, its stream stops halfway. It's as if there's an invisible bowl in the shape of an orb that the starlight fills. The white circle floats in the air. The Keeper smirks at me as the starlight floats into the air with the flick of her finger.

"You'll need to be more careful than that, Moon."

Dread blooms in the pit of my stomach. I watch as she opens her mouth. It's like she dislocates her jaw. It widens more than it ever should. The orb of starlight tips over, and the liquid light trickles down her throat. I gulp, taking one and then two steps backward. Something tells me that I should *run*, but as much as I try, I can't get myself to look away. She finishes the orb of light and snaps her teeth shut with a grin.

Nothing happens for an entire three seconds, before I start to see it. Her pale skin becomes paler until it's an icy white. Her skin is glowing from the inside out.

I turn around, slipping out of her grip when she tries to grab my arm. I run, faster and harder than I ever have, a stitch burning in my side. I'm too afraid to look over my shoulder. I only hear the screeches, the pounding of footsteps. I recognize the hall I'm in, then race past the sitting room and down the stairs and to the main entryway. I find a familiar door and leap through the barrier and out the pyramid, across the drawbridge, and into the city. Beings have all stopped in the streets, cars and rickshaws paused in the road. Everyone is looking up and pointing, so even as I keep running, I look up, too . . . then slow to a stop. There's a shadow like an enormous cloud filling the sky. I've never seen clouds in the sky here before, not once—and from the reactions of everyone around me, I don't think they've ever seen clouds here before, either. There are murmurs, whispers.

A lizard runs to my foot, up my leg, and to my shoulder. "Wolf!"

I'm here. He scampers down my arm, sitting in the palm of my hand.

"Where were you? Where did you go?"

The Keeper blocked me from coming within a certain radius of her, he tells me. *So when she waited for you in the field . . .* He looks up at the shadow of darkness that's almost completely covered the sky now.

"I did it," I tell him, tears rising. "I gave her the starlight, and Wolf—you should've seen her, it was like she was turning into something *else*, and now—"

Breathe, child.

"You were right. I never should have helped her."

You made a mistake. That's all.

"Do you hate me now?"

I could never hate you, Moon. He turns in my palm to face me again. *I have a favor I must ask of you. You need to leave. You need to leave this realm, and you need to promise me that you'll never come back again.*

"What?" I shake my head. "Why?"

Wolf doesn't have a chance to answer my question. The air gets so cold so quickly that my breath becomes steam. A wind begins to rush and howl.

"Is it her? Is it the Keeper?"

Wolf jumps from my hand and transforms into his favorite form. His powerful large, black body stands over me, protecting me and cutting the cold wind in half. *Oh, little Moon,* Wolf says. *You know that I will always be here for you. I will always offer my words and my love. But you already know that I was never meant to save you.*

I shake my head. I don't know what he means.

Did you know that you are already more powerful than you could have ever imagined? Wolf asks me. *You don't have any idea, do you, child? That you are made of wonders.*

Through his legs, I can see the beings around us who start to run. Some scream and others hide. *I'm sorry, Moon. I know this will be hard for you. But you'll need to go on without me.*

A light begins to glow from the pyramid's walls.

Return, Moon. Now!

I squeeze shut my eyes.

SAGE

I gasp like I was drowning and I've just burst through the water's surface. I'm in your world again, sitting in my bed, tears already in my eyes and wetting my cheeks.

I have to go back.

I clamp my eyes shut. I try to force myself out of my body. I try to *rise*, to jump *up*, but nothing happens. I have to go back to Wolf, to help him and make sure he's okay. What has the Keeper done? What if she hurts him, and everyone else? But I've used too much energy. My body won't let me leave again. I groan in frustration.

The sun is starting to come up, and any second now my mom will knock on my door, telling me it's time to get ready for school. I don't want to go. I can't imagine sitting at a desk in a pod, listening to a teacher right now. I'll only be able to think about Wolf, worried that he might be hurt. The thought alone makes me want to curl into a ball. I have to wait to return tomorrow night, but it'll be another fifty years by then. Who knows what will have happened to Wolf and everyone else in the spirit realm?

I take one big, shaky breath and try to release it slowly, the way my mom taught me to do whenever I'm afraid or overwhelmed. Breathe in for six seconds. Breathe out for six seconds. She told me about box breathing, too. Take in a breath for four seconds. Hold for four seconds. Let it out slowly for four seconds. Pause for four seconds. I keep doing this until I can feel my heart start to slow down in my chest. *Breathe, Moon,* she'd told me as I cried. *Breathe.*

★

My mom doesn't realize anything is wrong when she pushes my door open. "Time for school, baby." I shake my head. She walks inside and puts a hand to my forehead. She frowns. "You're not sick. And you just missed class yesterday," she says. "I'm sorry, Moon. You have to go today."

Why did we decide that someone has to have a fever to stay home? Why can't it be that, if we're not feeling well emotionally, we can stay in bed until we feel better again? We're not our bodies. Our bodies are borrowed from the earth, like plants growing from the ground, walking and talking and moving around. And when we die, our bodies go back to the earth again, and we leave this world and its realm. It isn't fair that so many people decide physical illness is the only one that matters. But there's so much about your world that isn't fair.

I drag myself out of bed, and I notice it just as I'm getting dressed.

Right there, right on my index finger—or, really, where my finger is supposed to be.

Light shines through, and I can see the wooden floorboards of my bedroom floor as if my finger was cut off and I didn't even notice it.

I touch my two fingers together. The skin is still there, pressing against my fingertips.

I just can't *see* it.

I'm spinning in circles, like I can suddenly feel Earth moving beneath my feet as it whirls around our solar system and galaxy.

I blink, and my brown skin is back again.

Am I even awake? Am I just dreaming?

That isn't possible. That's never happened before. I've never gone invisible while I'm still in your world.

★

Ever since the Keeper pointed at my throat and made me speak, I've been forgetting that I don't want to talk out loud anymore. I catch myself once or twice now, almost opening my mouth to say sorry when I accidentally kick Lilah underneath the desk, or when Wiley asks to borrow a pencil and says, "Thanks!" and I almost say, "You're welcome."

I don't want to speak. I tell myself this in my head. I don't like that the Keeper has taught me how to speak again. She's evil, isn't she? She proved it when she drank the light from the star. If she wanted me to learn to speak again, it couldn't have been for a good reason.

The last new classmate in my class's pod arrived a few days ago. He's quiet, though not as quiet as I am, which I guess isn't saying much, since I still don't speak.

"You're so lucky you missed class," Lilah tells him.

His name is Andrew. He has lighter brown skin and curly dark brown hair and dark brown eyes. He stares at his sneakers without saying anything, and for a second

I wonder if Andrew might be a little more like me—someone who doesn't like to talk with their voice, who isn't always sure if this world is reality—but then a grin lights up his face and he answers Lilah.

"It was kind of cool," he says. "Except the being sick part. And I still have to make up all the homework. That kind of sucks."

I'm watching Andrew so closely that I'm not looking at my hand when I pick up my pencil and my journal. When I look down again, my hand is completely gone.

I gasp and drop the pencil. It clatters to my desk and rolls off to bounce around on the floor. Wiley bends over to pick it up and reaches it out to me, waiting for me to take it, but I can't. I hide my invisible hand in my lap beneath my shirt as I stare at the pencil while he stares at me, brow raised. Heat rises to my neck and my cheeks.

Andrew reaches out and takes the pencil, then puts it on the desk in front of me. I blink as I stare at it. Wiley makes a face at him. It's a face I know well. I've seen it so many times from my classmates at my other school. It's a laugh and a smirk and a raised eyebrow. Wiley might as well say it out loud. I know what he's thinking. *Moon is so weird.*

I can feel my hand. I know it's still there. But when I glance at it from beneath my shirt, the skin fades in and out, light glimmering through, before it reappears again.

I can't pay attention in class. I don't even want to.

What if, one second, my entire head disappears? Then what would I do?

I don't even know why this is happening. Why is this happening?

Wolf would know. He always knows.

The teacher lectures from the screen on the wall. She talks to us and all the other pods about history and social studies. She tells us about all the wars this world has seen, over and over and over again. The same cycles, unbreaking. Why hasn't this world learned from the past's mistakes? I wonder if it's possible. World peace. Adults like to roll their eyes at the thought. They snort and shake their heads. Why? If every human in the world finds peace inside themselves, wouldn't that solve all your world's problems? Maybe then people wouldn't want to hurt others so badly, if they weren't hurting so much, and if they weren't so afraid. Afraid of other people and even afraid of themselves. Maybe then they wouldn't hate anyone who was different, and they would decide to love everyone else. I could be loved in a world like this. Loved by strangers instead of hated by people who don't know me because they're too afraid of what they don't understand. I wonder if that's possible. I think it might be. And maybe I can begin with myself.

ALOE VERA

I've always loved trees, even when I was young, younger than I am now. I can hear them speak. Their leaves flitter in the breeze, yellow and green shimmering and dancing in the light, and I can hear their titters and whispers. The old oaks with branches that curve and carve through the blue sky—they are wise, watching with proud silence, understanding so much, and understanding most that it's okay to not understand anything at all.

I wasn't so surprised when Wolf first told me that there's a tree growing inside my body. I can feel the roots reaching for the dirt, the buds trying to flower around my rib cage, the trunk lengthening through my spine, the branches and leaves crowning from the top of my head, matching the curve of my thick hair, a halo of black curls. If I have a tree inside me, do trees have humans inside their bodies? Maybe the spirits that trees have were once human, too. I think that's why I love trees so much. They live and grow and know that the lines that separate us aren't real or true.

My mom gave me a book about plants for my birthday last year. I like studying the scientific names and facts about the different herbs and flowers and fruit that grow around the world. There are so many plants that are used as medicine. Did you know? Cures for headaches and stomachaches, and even medicines for heartaches, too. I haven't found the right plant, yet—the one that would cure my sadness. Maybe the only one that can heal me is the tree that's still growing inside me. It's interesting, isn't it? That tree branches and leaves look like pictures of the inside of a brain, which look a lot like images of faraway galaxies.

ROSEMARY

When I get home from school, my mother tells me that
Mr. Richmond will no longer be my therapist, and that's
all she says about it, since she still isn't speaking to me
much anymore, on account of the fact that I'm not speaking to her—but in her silence, I can hear her thoughts.
There's no helping someone like me. If even my mom
and Mr. Richmond have given up, then there really isn't
any hope, right? Maybe my mom realized how pointless
it is, to keep paying money for me to sit down and stare,
knowing I will never be happy.

These are all the thoughts that spring through my
brain, so I'm surprised when I walk into the living room
and find a woman sitting there. My mom said that
Mr. Richmond would no longer be my therapist, but not
that he wouldn't be replaced.

"Hello, Moon," the woman says.

She's the sort of brown that echoes the richness of skin that's survived for thousands of years, with a smile that reminds me of lemons and peppermint tea and summer rain. "I'm Stella. Isn't that funny," she says. "Stella means *star* in Latin. Seems like we were meant to be friends."

I just want to go to my room and sit on my bed and close my eyes. I need to get back to Wolf—make sure he's all right. But Ms. Stella watches me expectantly. I sit down slowly. My mom is in the kitchen, keys jingling and papers rustling, getting ready to leave for her shift.

"Your mom thought it would be best for me to introduce myself," Ms. Stella says. "She's in a hurry. I know she'd have wanted to introduce the two of us if she could."

My mom must be even more mad than I thought. She doesn't even say goodbye as she opens the door, walks out, and slams it shut, locking it behind her.

Ms. Stella doesn't have a clipboard or a pen. She wears a dress that covers her knees and those inch-high black heels that remind me of what choir women wore in church when my mom used to make me go with her every Sunday morning. Ms. Stella looks like she's just about my mom's age, maybe even a little younger, and she's heavyset with a short-cropped Afro.

"You don't speak much," Ms. Stella says. "That's okay, because I can speak enough for the both of us. Your mom wasn't sure if Mr. Richmond was the best fit, and he didn't think so, either. It isn't because of you, or anything you did," she says. "Sometimes it just works out that way, doesn't it?"

She watches me then, silently, her own eyes narrowed like she's mimicking the expression on my face, soft smile growing. "Well, then," she says. "I suppose this is the moment we both fall into a comfortable silence."

We sit there, watching each other. I wait for Ms. Stella's expression to change—for any annoyance or impatience, before her eyes become glazed and I can get to know her a little more. But her expression stays exactly the same. She doesn't even look away. She keeps smiling, eyebrows rising with some expectation whenever I meet her eye, tilting her head a little when I look away again. I become more and more agitated and restless and annoyed. I can't sit still, not with her smiling at me like that, as if she's trying to prove a point. I don't know which point she's trying to prove. Maybe that I'm not the only one who can sit as silent and as long as I do.

The half hour drags on until finally she looks up at the clock on the wall. "That was quick, wasn't it?" she says. "Your mom's going to have some afternoon shifts for a while, so maybe I should try to talk to her about making this session an hour instead. Same price, not that you have to hurt your head about that."

I squint at her. I know what she's trying to do. She knows that the half hour was torture, so she wants to trap me with her for even longer until I finally break and start talking again. It doesn't matter. I'm up for the challenge.

Ms. Stella says that she'll just let herself out. She gets up, swiping off the back of her dress from the static of the couch, and tells me to have a very good day. I stay stuck on the sofa, even after I hear the door open and shut.

EUPHRASIA

I lie awake in my bed, staring at the ceiling, waiting for the time on my clock to click to three in the morning, which is when I know most people will be asleep. It'll be easier to leave my body then. I don't often get a lot of sleep. I heard once that a lack of sleep can lead to hallucinations. Sometimes I worry that the spirit world isn't even real. That it's just a story I've made up in my head with a bunch of different characters, same way I write about Blue in my journals, or that it's one dream I return to again and again.

The clock reads 2:36 a.m., but my eyes are heavy. I close them, and I can see the lights that swirl through the spirit world's night, the purples and greens that shine. I fall through the air, drifting through a forest floor. This isn't the same place I always come when I enter the spirit world, is it? Leaves tickle my cheeks, and branches pull at my hair as I glide past them. I land on dirt slicked by grass and the petals of flowers that rain down from above. It's nighttime, but the sky is illuminated by its shifting colors.

"Wolf?" I shout, my voice echoing. "Wolf, are you there?"

He told me not to come back to the spirit realm, but I never thought he would ignore me like this. He has always found me as soon as I call.

I wander the woods, looking for any sign of him—a paw print, branches above snapped in the shape of a giant wolf's ears. I've always believed that, even if no one else cares about me, at least he loves me. He's said so, time and again. *I love you, little one. Don't ever forget that. I love you, simply because you exist, and every soul in this grand universe of ours deserves to be loved and cherished. There are people who don't even know you and love you already, simply because you live, and you feel a pain they have felt.*

And that is when the cries begin.

I stop short, breath hitched. A branch cracks beneath my foot, and I put a hand on the rough bark of a tree, standing close. I love trees, but the bark isn't as warm and comforting as Wolf's fur. The Shadow's cries are so deep that they vibrate in my chest, yet the wailing is high-pitched, like a baby's cry that's stretched out, faded and muffled and *wrong*. It's wrong, this sound. The hollow sobs echo through the air, which is much colder now, prickling my skin even though I'm sweating with fear. There's silence. Maybe the monster didn't realize I'm here.

This is what I hope for, what I tell myself—but then there's one piercing cry, so sharp and loud that it's more like a scream. I gasp, spinning around, expecting to see the monster there right in front of me. Here and now, I can feel the eyes of someone—*something*—unseen, watching me.

What will the monster do if it catches me?

Will I just wake up, or will I be caught in a nightmare?

My heart races in my chest. There's a rustling, and I turn around so fast that my foot slips on the flower petals beneath. I fall hard to the dirt. The cries grow into high-pitched laughter that rings in my ears, and suddenly, it isn't only one voice. There are dozens of laughs ricocheting through the trees. The laughter isn't the friendly kind. There are whispers. *Everyone hates you, Moon.*

And I begin to see the smoky haze, too. It's the same that follows the monster wherever it goes. It looks like the smoke of incense curling and unfurling through the air, ash rising from a firepit. The monster is so dark that I can see only its outline in the shadows.

Moon.

Its voice is just a whisper.

I scramble backward. I want to cry for Wolf, but I already know he isn't coming. I squeeze my eyes shut, trying to force myself to return to your world.

Moon.

The shadows are drifting closer, the smoke blocking out the lights from above.

"What do you want from me?" I yell, but the monster doesn't answer me. "Why do you follow me everywhere I go?"

The black hole that's usually inside me grows.

"Moon."

I open my eyes. I'm in my bedroom, though it's still night. The sky is a dark blue, the color before dawn. My mom sits on the edge of my bed, her hand on my shoulder, shaking me gently, bags beneath her eyes. She must be so tired.

"Moon, honey," she says. "You were having a bad dream."

A dream.

It was only a dream.

I wasn't in the spirit world at all.

I didn't even leave my body.

I've always been able to return to the spirit world, at least once a night. Why wasn't I able to now, when I needed to most of all?

I nod and swallow and turn my back to my mom so that she won't see the tears growing in my eyes. She waits there, her hand still lingering in the air, like she wants to ask me what my nightmare was about, or maybe to ask if I'm going to be all right, but she only stands up with a sigh. She goes to the door and shuts off the light.

LOTUS

I go to my pod and sit silently at my table while Lilah and Wiley and Andrew ignore me.

My skin goes in and out and in again.

I stare out the window, and I try not to dream.

I sit at my desk. My mom's voice sounds far away.

"I called your psychiatrist today," she says.

My journal is open, a pen in my hand. Maybe I'll disappear completely.

"I thought it might be time to try your prescription again," my mom tells me. "Are you listening, Moon?"

She leans against my desk so that she's in my line of vision. "I'm worried about you. Everything about the world is scary right now. I want to give you a higher dose, to help with any bad feelings. Okay?"

I shake my head. I don't want to take medication. I tried the pills once, many months ago. It just makes everything cloudy and fuzzy and easy to forget.

"We'll try it out again, just for a little while. It'll be good for you, Moon."

I don't think that's true. Prescriptions have helped many people, and Mr. Richmond told me he knows a lot of children who have been helped by antidepressants, but I'm not one of them. Whenever anyone acts like medication should have worked for me, I feel even more alone—as if prescriptions have helped every single person with depression except for me. As if there's something so wrong with me that I'm broken beyond repair. Wolf says that I'm not broken, but why does the world treat me like I am? Why do they expect medication to help me, as if my truth doesn't matter, too?"

My mom takes a breath. "I was . . . sad, once," she says. "It was when I was just about your age. Thirteen years old. My mom was very religious and strict. I wasn't allowed to go out, not the way other girls in my class could. I wasn't allowed to wear the kinds of clothes people said were cool. I got made fun of every single day. I went to church, and I went to class, and I just waited— waited to grow up so that I could get away and escape." Her smile fades. "I don't know why I'm telling you this.

It's not the same, not at all. I was depressed, and I was anxious, but I never . . ."

She doesn't know how to finish that sentence. And for the first time in a long while, she doesn't try to finish it, either. She only sits with me. She breathes. And I get to know her in the silence, more than she would normally let me. My mom works with death. She looks people in the eye, knowing they're soon going to die. I wonder what that must be like. Does this make her realize how fragile life can be? Does she look at me and realize how easily she could lose me?

"It's a miracle, when you think about it," she says. "It's a miracle, to be alive. I try so hard to figure out just the right thing to say, to make you better—to make you feel loved, to know that I want you here, to help you want to live and laugh and speak again, and every day that I fail, I think it must be because I'm a bad mother, to not know what to say and—"

My mom is crying. I saw her cry only once, long ago, when my father yelled at her. He raised his hand like he was going to hit her, and then he left, storming out the door. My mom cried as she explained that he didn't want us anymore. We weren't good enough for him to stay. No tears actually fall this time. They only build in her eyes, shining in the light. She takes a quick, sharp breath through her nose and blinks and sits up straight. "But maybe there isn't anything I can do or say. It has to be up to you to find your happiness. If you tried—just *try*, Moon. Think different thoughts. Act differently from the way you do."

Act different. *Be* different. Don't be a child that makes my mom ashamed. I bet she pictured someone else when she found out she was making another human being, bringing me out of the spirit world and into this one. She didn't realize I would be so depressed, so frustrating. If she did, she would have said, "Never mind. Why would I ever want this child?"

"I'm sorry, Moon. I didn't mean it like that. I meant—just try to talk. Try to laugh. Try to smile. You'll see. Things aren't as bad as you've made them out to be."

There doesn't even have to be a reason for it sometimes. Everything will be the way it usually is, and then I feel the universe expanding in my chest, black hole growing. The only way I know how to get out of the black hole when it's still daytime—to get out of my universe, my world, myself—is to sit down with a journal and my pen and start to write again. Characters and their stories let me escape my thoughts and my body and the sadness that traps me there. Blue is sad, too. Maybe even sadder than me. She wants to go back to the sky so badly.

But it's harder to write, the longer I've been away from the world of the spirits. Words don't come to me as easily, and images don't fill my mind, not like they once did.

My mom is gone. She hasn't been beside me for some time. She must've given up.

THYME

My mom leaves for her shift right after I'm back from school. She's been leaving earlier and earlier these days, as if she can't wait to get away. I've tried to close my eyes and leave my body many times, but it's no use when so many people in the city are still awake.

I walk into the living room and almost jump out of my skin.

Ms. Stella is already there. She's wearing a bright pink dress today with the same black, one-inch heels. "Hello, Moon," she says brightly, as bright as her name sounds.

She gestures at the sofa opposite her. I want to groan. I forgot about therapy. I don't want to have to sit here and try to hide that my skin is going invisible on top of everything else.

But she's watching me expectantly, so I move to sit

down across from her. I sink into the couch and look at her as she looks at me.

She smiles. "How're you doing today?"

Her smile doesn't waver, not for one second, not even when I don't answer her. I almost want to ask her how she can be so happy all the time. I want to ask her if it's just a lie she puts on for the world.

When people want me to be happy, I think it's because they're uncomfortable with the fact that I'm sad. It's the same reason why, when someone asks, "How are you?" with a smile, all they want to hear is "Good!" even though most of the time we're not really okay at all. If you actually say how you're feeling, people will look at you like you're weird.

I would know. I've done it before. Once, before the Long Hot Summer, I said, "I'm having a really bad day," when my teacher asked me how I was doing, just because I was curious to see what she would say. She just nodded and turned away.

Why do we have to lie about something like that? If I'm expected to just lie and pretend to be happy so that everyone else will be comfortable, then I don't think there's any point to me saying anything at all.

"I'm doing pretty well myself," Ms. Stella says. The hand that's been fading in and out is still hidden in my pocket, but when I clutch my other hand in my lap, I look down and see that it's starting to get a lighter shade of brown, too.

Ms. Stella says, "I thought that today I might talk about some things I wish I'd known when I was your age."

I hate when adults get like this. I hate when they think they have the right words to say, when they think I'm just being dramatic or immature because I'm younger than they are—as if I don't have any real feelings until I officially become eighteen years old, as if none of my thoughts even matter. Maybe that's more about adults and how they want to feel, too.

"I wish I'd known that there's so much that we humans don't understand," she tells me. "I would spend most of my time sitting in the woods behind my father's house, in Virginia where I grew up. I would spend days out there if I could, just sitting with the trees and listening to them whisper to me. My dad once asked me, 'Stella, what in the world are you doing out there in those woods all day?' And I told him, 'I'm listening to the trees.' And he said, 'Don't be silly, Stella. Trees can't speak.'

"And I had so much shame inside of me, so much embarrassment that I didn't know a simple thing like that, that I stopped listening to the trees, and I stopped spending my days out there in those woods. But there's so much that we don't understand about this world. Who's to say those trees weren't whispering their secrets, Moon?" Ms. Stella says, "I think most times adults can mean the best, and they can love you so, so much, but sometimes we make mistakes because we're humans, too. We make mistakes because of what our own parents did or said, which are mistakes that are carried on from generation to generation inside of us, deep in our skin. I think my dad must have had a friend himself, when he was young—someone or something that no one else could see. And an adult probably told him to stop fooling around, to be practical, to think that only the things he could see are real."

Inside the black hole in my chest, there is the other side that scientists don't understand yet. We don't understand black holes. We don't know why it is that light disappears and why life and matter and everything else ceases to exist. I start to wonder—maybe there's some light in there, if I look deep enough. Maybe there's an entirely different galaxy and universe, similar to our own.

"Your mother loves you very much, Moon," Ms. Stella tells me. "She loves you more than anything and anyone in this world."

I want to ask Ms. Stella how she knows something like that.

How does she know?

She doesn't see the way my mom looks at me, the way my mom talks to me. Ms. Stella doesn't feel the regret I feel inside my mom whenever we're even in the same room.

"But your mom will make mistakes," Ms. Stella tells me, "because mistakes were made with her, too. I think what's beautiful is that we all have the chance to heal from those mistakes. We could even be grateful, though you don't have to be if you don't want to."

Grateful, for the fact that my mother doesn't love me?

"Grateful," Ms. Stella says, as if she heard my question out loud, "for the chance to grow—to heal those mistakes that were made with you, and with her. How wonderful is that, Moon? It's almost like there's a tree inside of you. You planted a seed when you were born, and throughout your life, lessons are learned, and that tree starts to grow and grow and grow. Roots, tangled in the earth. Leaves, always stretching for the light."

I wonder what mistakes were made with my mom. What it is that could've happened to her, to make her the sort of person she is today?

I wonder what lessons she needed to learn, and if she ever learned them.

And I think about the lessons I need to learn, too. It isn't enough to know that I want to stop being afraid. How do I actually become that person?

I have so many questions I want to ask Ms. Stella, but my voice keeps bubbling and breaking, swallowing down the words.

Ms. Stella's smile hasn't stopped, not once, but it's softer now—more thoughtful as she watches me. "You're an incredible child, Moon," she says.

Why does she think something like that, something that couldn't be further from the truth?

"You're an incredible child because all children are incredible. You still have so many choices to make in your life. We adults," she says, with the smallest laugh, "it's so easy to get set in our ways. We get something in our head and we think that's exactly how the world is, and there's no changing it. We could change so much, heal and grow so much, too, if we wanted to, but so many of us are afraid. Because of that fear, we get set in our ways and we stop healing and stop growing and stop changing the world. But you—you, and children like you, have the magic to shape the entire universe."

Ms. Stella stands up then, and I look at the clock on the wall in surprise. It's already been a full hour of Ms. Stella talking and watching, even though it feels like it's been only five minutes.

"It's always wonderful to see you, Moon," she says, and I stay in my seat until I hear the door open and close behind her. And even then, I stay exactly where I am— thinking of Ms. Stella's words, wishing I could feel them in my heart and not just in my head.

★

I got so lost in thought, sitting there on that couch, that I'm surprised when the door opens again. I hear the jingle of keys as my mom walks in the door in a flurry. I can feel her exhaustion as she marches into the living room.

"Moon?" she says, surprised. "What're you doing, sitting here in the dark?"

She flips on the light, brightness glaring into my eyes. "It's getting late. Did you eat the food I left for you in the fridge? Did you do your homework?" She walks into the living room, clearing up the coffee table—picking up a glass, the photo albums I never look at, and the magazines. "It's like I'm talking to myself," she whispers. "I just don't know what to do sometimes. What can I do? I don't know how to try."

My mom straightens with a sigh. "It's getting late, Moon," she says. "Come on. Let's get to bed."

I know I don't have to speak, not if I don't want to—but I think I want to speak now. I don't even know what to say. I make the smallest sound, and my mom doesn't stop walking. I'm not sure if she's even heard me. I try again.

"I—"

My voice is soft, like a whisper. My mom once said it sounds like the beginning of a lullaby. She stops and looks over her shoulder, like she isn't sure if she's imagining that she heard right, or if my voice was just a sound in her head. I'm not sure of the answer to that one myself. She stops breathing, and everything stills. With her eyes on me, watching with so much gravity weighing me down to the earth, my mind becomes a blank field of white snow.

"What?" she says, breathless. "You what?"

I shake my head, my mouth squeezing shut.

"You what?" she says again. "You what? Speak, Moon—say what you were going to say."

I can't look at her, not with so much disappointment and desperation in her eyes. I can feel how much she wants to reach out to me, to take my hands and wrap me in her arms like she did when I was young, still so unhurt by this world, still so willing to be alive. She doesn't try to stop me when I leave her standing there, watching me go. She's never known how to stop me, how to make me stay in your world.

Blue was often sad, too. Her name was perfect because her happiness was like the phases of the moon: sometimes bright and full, shining yellow light; other times a pale shadow, only half there, a blueness that cloaked them; still others, there was nothing at all but darkness, and no hope in sight.

The Magician did what they could to make Blue happy. They gave Blue a home in the apothecary, which was a pretty fun place to live. They both shared one room on the top floor, where the Magician would make breads and cakes. The air always smelled like flour and sugar and cinnamon. The Magician's paintings were hung up all over the wall, and there were plants everywhere, too: vines that unfurled and flowers that would snap shut whenever Blue tried to touch them. There were instructions for alchemic potions and recipes for strawberry-rhubarb tarts and a bunch of other papers in stacks that always looked like they were just about to tip over, though they never did, and books everywhere—on the shelves, on piles on the floor, in Blue's hands.

Blue loved to read. Books were magical portals in this world, you see. There are some stories in our own world, about wardrobes and mirrors that can take someone and put them into a whole other universe. These portals are always hard to find. But in Blue's world, everyone knew that the portals were as easy to find as walking into a bookstore. Blue would open a book just so she could visit another world. Sometimes she would even come to yours. She would wander the streets of the city, amazed by the towers of steel and glass, some as tall as mountains. She would jump back in fright at the honking yellow animals that had no legs, only wheels. She would taste the strange meat that was placed between two pieces of bread and smothered in a red and yellow sauce. Yes, this world was very weird to Blue! And she was always happy to go back home again.

The apothecary shop was downstairs, with a little bell that jingled whenever someone opened the door. The shelves were filled with jars of the weirdest, grossest stuff: squirrel tails and shark eyes and toenails and little baby teeth. (Blue preferred not to think where the Magician had found those.) And there was a jar of wishes, too. The pearls glowed even in the dark, long after the shop was closed and when Blue was supposed to be fast asleep. Blue wondered what would happen if she held the entire jar up to the sky and begged the star to take her home. Because no matter what the Magician did to make her happy, the phases of the moon would come again, and the light would fade until there was nothing left.

On a night that had no light, Blue sneaked downstairs while the Magician slept and picked up the jar of wishes. She clasped it in her hand as she opened the jingling door. She stood in the garden, where she'd been brought twelve years before, and she looked the star right in the eye and held that jar up to the sky.

"Please," she said. "Please take me home. No matter what I do, I'm not happy. The happiness comes and goes, but I'll always be sad again. I think it's because I don't belong here. I'm supposed to be in the sky. I'm supposed to be a star, too."

But it didn't matter how many wishes Blue offered. The star would not take her home again. The Magician had woken up to the sound of the jingling door and followed Blue to the garden. They'd heard Blue's words. They were so deeply hurt that the child they loved wanted to leave them behind to become a star in the sky.

PITAYAH

I sit in my bed, eyes sore, trying not to cry in frustration. It's 3:33 in the morning. This is the second night in a row that I haven't been able to leave my body. Maybe it's the pressure that's getting to me, and the fear—all the worry I have for Wolf getting in my head and blocking me from returning. By the time I get back, it'll have been at least over one hundred years, maybe more. Who knows what will have happened?

And I just happen to look out my window.

And there, far beneath and standing on the other side of the street, is the child.

I'd seen them once before, on my way to school, when I chased them into the park. I'd thought that maybe the child had been only a dream or a piece of my imagination, but here they are—standing in the street, staring at things I can't see, as if awed by a world of magic. I pinch my arm, and I'm as awake as I've ever been, and this time—yes, this time, I know for a fact that they're real.

I leap to my feet and I race out the apartment door, Christmas bells giggling behind me. I burst out the apartment lobby doors and into the street.

I skid to a stop. The child's eyes widen when they see me.

I stare at them, and they stare at me.

And then, with absolutely no warning at all, they turn on their heel and race away—run so fast they might as well be flying.

I sprint after them, my feet slapping the sidewalk's concrete.

The sky is purple and dark blue as we run into the park. The park is different at night. There are even more shadows that seem to move in the moonlight, and the cicadas must be asleep. It's still just as hot, though, sweat sticking to me as I push through the roots and thorns and leaves. My mom won't like it if she finds out that I left the apartment. Did she hear the bells ringing? Has she walked to the open door and realized I'm gone?

But I've never seen a spirit come into your world, and

my curiosity is like fire, catching on to anything that's too close and burning right through me. I follow the child until I reach a clearing. I stop, surprised. The child has vanished.

I hear a voice echo in my mind. *Why are you chasing me?*

"I'm sorry. I didn't mean to scare you. I was just curious."

Curious?

"I won't hurt you. It's okay to come out again."

There, behind a tree—I see a faint light fading into sight, and the child peeks at me from around the trunk with their big eyes.

"How can you see me?" the child asks. "No one here has ever seen me before."

I walk a little closer, slowly. I don't want to scare them off again. "I don't know. I think it's because I spend so much time in the spirit realm."

Their eyebrows rise with surprise. "You've been to the spirit realm before?"

"I usually go every night to the city," I say. "But . . . something's happened. I haven't been able to return."

The child steps out from behind the tree fully now.

Their scales glimmer in the dim light. "That's probably for the best. The city is dangerous. Not everyone made it out, and it's hard to go back again."

My heart clenches. "What happened?"

"The Keeper," they tell me. "She changed. The city is under her control, and she did something to the spirits still trapped with her."

Wolf and all the others are stuck there, and it's my fault. It's because I helped her get the starlight and the power that she wanted.

The child keeps talking. "I was lucky. I wasn't there when she used her spell. I was here, in the world of the living, even though I'm not supposed to be." It's as if the more they talk, the less shy they are. "Hey," they say suddenly. "What's your name? I've had a ton of names before. It's probably easier if you just call me Dragon."

My voice sounds hollow, even to me. "I'm Moon."

Dragon steps forward, concern in their frown. "Are you okay, Moon?"

"I have a friend trapped in the city with the Keeper," I tell them, "and I can't even go back to see if they're okay."

"It really is probably for the best," they say again. "The Keeper might trap you there with her, too."

"I don't care. I have to figure out a way to go back."

They're hesitant, but then they say, "Maybe I can help."

★

Dragon tries to explain the way energy and vibrations and frequencies work, but it just makes my head spin. I decide to trust them when they say that I might not be able to get to the spirit realm on my own, but I will be able to return with them. I sneak back into the apartment. Luckily, my mom didn't wake up, even with the bells ringing. Dragon follows me, eyes wide.

"This is how human beings live now?"

I'm desperate to get back to the spirit realm, but maybe their curiosity is contagious. "When was the last time you were alive?"

"It's been a very, *very* long time." Dragon stares around my room when I open the door. Am I just imagining the sadness in their eyes? "I was supposed to return to the higher realms," they tell me. "I wasn't supposed to be in the city at all, and I'm certainly not supposed to be in your world again."

"It isn't my world," I mutter.

They tilt their head. "But it's the world of the living. You're alive, aren't you? I wish I was," they say.

I frown. "Why would you wish that? Everyone hurts each other here. There's so much pain and sadness."

They seem thoughtful. "Yes, that's true. But there's so much peace and joy, too. When you look up through the trees and see the sunlight shining through the leaves. When you hear a beautiful song, so pretty that it makes you want to cry. When the breeze blows against your cheek. That feeling—I wouldn't trade that feeling for the world. It's the feeling you get when you realize the future isn't real, and neither is the past, and the only thing that exists at all is this one moment, right now. That feeling of peace."

I know the kind of moment Dragon is talking about—those moments where it feels like all of life's happiness and love and joy is pulled into one heartbeat. But I don't know if those seconds balance out all the bad ones. I've spent too many nights crying myself to sleep to think it'd be worth it to stay alive just for those few moments of peace. Wolf's voice echoes in my head. *Wait and see.* Wait to see how it'll all balance out, how life will be worth it in the end.

I push Wolf's voice out of my mind. I've already wasted enough time, when I should be trying to get back to the spirit realm. It's almost five in the morning. My mom is going to come to wake me up in just a couple of hours.

"We should hurry," I tell them.

"Okay," Dragon says. "Close your eyes."

I do, and I breathe, and this time when I try to imagine going up, I feel a hand holding mine. I open my eyes again, and I see that Dragon is pulling me up from my body—pulling me into the air, through my bedroom's ceiling and into the sky, pink from the rising sun far on the horizon.

TURMERIC

The field is no longer a field but an entire forest. The trees are so tall that they scrape the top of this realm's sky. They're like giant redwoods, even bigger than any tree that's ever grown on Earth.

Dragon isn't surprised. "This is what it looked like, the last time I was here."

I realize they're looking right at me. I'm confused, until I look down at myself, too. My gold chain is still there, threaded around my ankle—but I can *see* my ankle. I'm still a little transparent, but I'm not as see-through as I am when I usually come. That can't be a good sign, can it? I'm going invisible in the world of the living, but I'm becoming more visible in the realm of the spirits. I think about the last time I was with the Keeper—how she kept me here, with her, even with my alarm blaring, and even after my body was totally solid.

Wolf has always warned that I should never stay in this realm long enough to become completely visible.

It's been two nights in the world of the living since I've returned. How much time has passed here? Five hundred years? A thousand? There are no lights in the city's outskirts. Trees grow right up to the last of the buildings, taller than the tallest skyscrapers. It's completely dark. Even the sky is still covered by a gray cloud that shifts and morphs like it's alive. The main source of light comes from the center of the city. The pyramid glows a faint gold. Every now and then, purple lightning strikes through the air. It illuminates the maze of streets, and when my eyes adjust to the dark, I see the city's remains.

The city is practically a wasteland now. It looks like ash is rising into the air. I hear a chorus of cries that echo across the sky. It almost sounds like the songs of whales beneath the sea. The cries go on and on, vibrating through my lungs. The sound alone makes my skin prickle, an ice cube sliding down my throat. What *is* that? What could ever make such a sad, sorrowful sound? The noise reminds me of my Shadow, always following, but there are so many more voices now. The stacks of homes with architecture from centuries ago crumble. A pagoda leans to the side, and a tower's glass is broken, skeletal concrete left behind. A coliseum looks like it would in your world, pillars falling apart into chunks of stone.

But that's not what grabs my attention. What grabs my attention—what I can't look away from at all—are the beings. They're lying down in the street, as if they're exactly where they fell more than a thousand years before. There is grass growing through the dirt, coming in from the field, and vines covering them, moss growing across their skin and scale and clothes, flowers blossoming.

"They're asleep," Dragon tells me. "That's the spell that the Keeper put on the realm. The spirits who have recently passed on wander, lost, unable to move into the higher realms. She captures them and puts them under her spell, too. We'll have to be really, really careful, Moon."

But there's only one thing on my mind. "I have to get to the pyramid."

"What? Didn't you listen to anything I said? She'll capture us if she sees us."

"We'll have to make sure she doesn't see us, then."

If none of these beings have moved since the last time

I was here, then Wolf can be in only one place. We sneak through the streets, Dragon grumbling behind me. "This is such a bad idea. We're going to be in so much trouble if she finds us." There's an old sail of a boat, flapping in the wind, and a stall I'd hidden behind once still has dishes laid out, beings asleep in their seats, heads on the counter or in their lunch.

There's a crack of thunder. "What is with that storm?" I whisper.

"I don't know," Dragon says. They stare up with a frown. I think they might be even more concerned than they really want to let on. "It's almost like it's alive, isn't it? Almost like a monster."

I wouldn't be able to handle a thunderstorm that's a monster on top of everything else, so I don't respond as we keep walking. I peer around an old theater, exactly like I did just this summer, and there—yes, I see him, right there beside the drawbridge. "*Wolf.*"

"Who?"

I ignore Dragon and look both ways before I cross the street, even though I should know that nothing is coming, and I run across to where Wolf lies. He's still in his big, black form. I slow to a stop as I reach him. His eyes are closed, and for a second, it looks like he isn't breathing—but then a slow and steady steam releases from his nostrils and his long muzzle where I see a glimmer of his large, sharp white teeth. He seems so powerful, even while he's asleep. His fur glistens as his chest rises and falls with every breath. Flowers have grown around his snout.

I put a hand against his dry, cracked nose. "Wolf. Wolf, please wake up."

Dragon pauses beside me. "Is that your friend?"

It's hard to swallow down the tears. "He isn't hurt, is he?"

"He's only asleep."

Wolf is the only friend I've ever had. I want to nestle into his fur and lie down beside him, even if that means staying here for the rest of eternity. "Wolf would know what to do. He would tell us how to help everyone. How to stop the Keeper." And he'd know how to help me, too. How to stop me from going invisible in your world.

Dragon frowns at the sky. The thunder rumbles louder, growing like a growl. "It's her. The Keeper. I think she knows we're here."

I bury myself deeper in Wolf's fur, but Dragon grabs

my arm. Just as I look up, I see a funnel—the start of a tornado, gray clouds thickening and swirling down to the tip of the pyramid.

"We have to go—now, Moon!"

They pull my hand, and faster than I've ever gone, even faster than when I was on Wolf's back, I rush forward, tugged along by Dragon as they fly through the air, zipping through and between fallen buildings. It's like they've given me some of their magic, too. My feet skate along on air, and I don't even feel out of breath. I look over my shoulder to see that the clouds have become like smoke, gushing through the alleyways and roads as it follows, wind screeching. The Shadow. It reminds me of the Shadow.

Dragon whooshes us out of the city, into the forest, and above the trees. They fly through the air, and I see that the gush of smoke has stopped far behind us, at the city's edge. Even then, Dragon doesn't stop. We soar over lands that have changed so much. The grassy fields where trees live now. The lakes and rivers and sea, dried into desert plains. The clouds fade away and the skies return to the colors I'm used to seeing here in the spirit world. There are galaxies swirling above us, pinks and blues and greens colliding, waves of energy materializing and flowing back and forth like the waves of the ocean, patterns opening and closing. We go so far, so fast, that I even begin to see mountains. Wolf has never taken me this far across the lands.

Maybe we need to be this far away for Dragon to feel safe from the Keeper. I know that, even here, I'm nervous that she'll still appear out of thin air. The Keeper reminds me of people in the world of the living. She reminds me of the kind of people who don't care about others, and who want to hurt someone else just because they're different. I wonder why anyone would want to hurt someone else, but maybe in the world of the living, their reasons are exactly the same as the Keeper's. Maybe in your world, people are trying to steal another person's soul in the same way—hoard them, drink from them, and make themselves feel more powerful because of what they have taken. But does that ever really make another person more powerful in the end?

Dragon slows down only when we reach a cliff on the edge of a mountain. It looks like the other end of the realm. I've never been to this side before. They puff out a breath. "That was a close call."

The mountain's stone is so pale that it almost looks like it's made of crystal. I think it might be, actually—a mountain of quartz. There's snow glittering on the ground, but it isn't cold when a breeze blows. I look over the edge of the cliff, down at the shimmering planes and reflections of your world.

"Now what?" I ask them. "We have to figure out how to stop the Keeper. The answer is probably in the city somewhere. We can't just run away."

"Why not?" they say with a shrug. "I run away all the time. I've turned out to be just fine."

Great. Dragon has helped me, and I know I should be grateful, but they're nothing like Wolf. I sit down, my knees to my chest, and stare out over the edge of the realm. "I'm disappearing in the world of the living," I tell them. "My skin has been turning see-through, and now my hand is completely gone. Well, it was," I say, holding it up for Dragon to see. "As soon as I walked into the spirit world, it came back again."

I can tell from Dragon's expression alone that this is not a good sign. "You were in the spirit world for too long," they tell me. "Part of your soul is intertwined with our world now. And now that you're back, the more intertwined with the world of the spirits you will become. You'll disappear from the world of the living completely."

"But what about the other side?" I say. "I can't walk around invisible like I'm a ghost. Wolf would know what to do. I have to figure out a way to wake him up. I have to stop the Keeper."

"To be honest, a part of me has been happy," Dragon says. "Because of the Keeper, no one can go to the higher realms. I haven't had to run away very much in the past thousand years. I've been able to stay here and visit your world as much as I like."

Anger bubbles up. "I told you, it's not my world. And how can you be happy when so many beings are hurting?"

They sit down beside me, legs swinging over the side of the cliff. Dragon apologizes, and I feel better when they actually do look a little sorry. "I don't mean to be selfish. I just miss living. I miss being alive."

"Why were you in the world of the living, anyway?" I ask them. "You said you'd gotten lost, but I saw you on the other side twice."

They hesitate, but then they say, "Fine, I'll admit it.

I like to visit whenever I can. But I could get in trouble for saying that. It's forbidden, going to the world of the living. I have to keep it a secret, but I can't help going back. The land of the living is such a beautiful place."

They don't want to be in the spirit world. They want to be in the land of the living instead. I feel bad for them. I know what it's like, to be in the wrong realm.

"Why do you like the world of the living?" I ask them.

"Who wouldn't want to be alive? The land of the living has so much magic."

I almost laugh. The land of the living, magical? "Are you sure you're thinking of the right place?"

"I've been in the spirit world for a really, really, *really* long time, and I can tell you that the land of the living is magical. Everything is still possible. People can do extraordinary things. They can grow, like a tree sprouting from a seed. A single person can change the world, even."

"Not always in a good way."

"No, not always. But don't you think that if someone has the power to create so much pain, someone else can also have the power to create so much love and hope and joy instead?"

"Why don't you just stay there, then?"

They shake their head. "A spirit on the other side? It wouldn't be living. Not really. Just as you're not living by staying here."

Dragon sounds like they've been around for such a long time. "How old are you?" I ask them.

"In this form? I think I'm about twelve," they say. "It's one of my favorite lives, so this is the form that I kept."

I wonder how many lives Dragon has lived. "How many forms have you had?"

"Way too many to count," they say. "I'm supposed to have ascended by now. My soul is very old. Not that that's important. It's more exciting to be a newer soul, I think, getting to experience life for the first time. There's still so much to learn."

I've heard similar words before. It feels like there's something important I should remember, tugging on the edges of my memory. "What have you learned?" I ask them.

They tilt their head as they watch me. "There was a life I had where I had to learn to love myself. A few lives where I had to learn how to love others. One where I had to stop working so much and enjoy my life. Another where I needed to learn how to feel free, without an ounce of fear in my body, not caring what anyone around me thinks. Most lives had multiple lessons, too, all of them intertwined. So many lessons can be learned in a lifetime. It's almost like characters in stories, isn't it? Every character has lessons to learn also. That's why there's so much conflict."

"Do you like to read, too?"

"Oh, yes," they say. "Reading was my favorite hobby. Almost every single one of my lives loved to read. Except Jack. Jack didn't like to read very much."

I can't help but laugh. Dragon is confusing, and they might just be as weird as me, but I also think I might like that.

"I wouldn't want to be a character in a story," I tell them. "That would have to mean conflict happens for a reason. I wouldn't want anyone to give me so much pain. The way people have treated me—bullies, even complete strangers." Those feelings that find me whenever I sit in silence. The thought that I don't want to be alive. "It just hurts. That's all. That's it. There isn't any purpose to it."

"That's the way it is for some people," Dragon says. "That's how it was for me, too, for a lot of the lives I lived. But there were some other lives that I had also. There were lessons I learned from the pain. I learned how to love myself, even when I wasn't being shown that love by anyone else. And because I knew how much that pain hurt, and because I knew what it was like to be mistreated and still turn to love anyway, I was able to help so many other people like me who were hurting also. I was able to turn that pain into something else. It was like magic. I was even able to show love to the people who hurt me. It wasn't something I ever had to do. It wasn't my responsibility to help people who had hurt me. But showing love turned out to be even more powerful than anything I'd ever experienced before. Because we're actually made of love, in the end, and anything that returns us to the purest form of our original state gives us power. Even more power than a star," they tell me. "I'd been a star, too, you know. It was fine, being a star, but I already knew that I was powerful when I was one. So to live a life where I'm lied to, and told that I'm not worthy of love, and learning that I am, always, no matter what, felt even more powerful."

I take a moment to think about Dragon's words, everything that they've said. Would I be able to forgive the people who treated me so badly? The people who hate me, without even knowing me? I don't know if I can show them love in return. And why should I? Like Dragon themself said, it isn't my responsibility—no, not at all. But would it help me? Help me to weave my pain into something else instead?

That's what I'm thinking of, when it sinks in just a little more that Dragon said they'd been a star. And just like that, the memory comes to me: the silhouette of silver light, the voice echoing. *There will be three.*

What had the star meant? They said that when the time comes, I'll need their help.

The first will be waiting. Ask for them, when you don't know what else to do.

"I met a star once," I tell Dragon. They glance up. "They told me that when I don't know what else to do, someone—or *something*—would be waiting to help me."

"Stars tend to be mysterious like that," Dragon tells me. "We can see all of time as one since time doesn't actually exist, but we're not allowed to give answers to others' questions. What would be the point, if you couldn't learn for yourself?"

"But I still don't know what the star meant." *The answer you need is inside you.* "What else did the star say?" I ask myself, trying to force my memory to work. It's like trying to pull details from a dream. "Calling for me. I think that someone will call for me, and I need to listen for them."

"Well," Dragon says, "maybe you should stop and listen."

It doesn't hurt to try. I take a breath, and I close my eyes. It feels like seconds, minutes, hours pass by. I get antsy with impatience and frustration. Is this working? It isn't working, is it?

The answer you need is inside you.

I realize that what I'd thought had been only the breeze is a whisper. I hear my name. *Moon.* I hear it, over and over again, in the hush of the waves of grass and with every breath.

You only have to listen for them. They will call your name when the time comes.

Dragon asks me a question, but I don't know what they say, because they're echoing as if they're far away.

ELM

I open my eyes again. There are grassy plains that look like they go on forever, maybe even longer than the sea. The fields are interrupted by a small, sloping hill—and I see, on top of the hill, a single tree.

No one else is around. Not even Dragon.

I wonder what they must think. One second, I'm beside them on a cliff, and the next second, I've completely vanished.

What else can I do? I hesitate, then begin to walk closer.

The tree is young and just as big as me. The leaves are a bright yellow, glimmering like stardust. They're so bright that the golden glitter shimmers and glows, rising slowly. I stop several feet away. I'm expecting someone to leap out from their hiding place, so I jump when a voice echoes.

Hello, Moon.

I stare. Is the tree talking to me?

There's a laugh. *You've experienced stranger things, haven't you?*

Yes, that's true, but . . . "Who are you?" I ask.

I've gone by many names. You can call me Joy. I'm one of your guardians.

I have guardians?

Joy must be able to hear my thoughts. *Every person in the world of the living has guardians*, they tell me. *Beings who watch over you from the spirit realm. They try to help you whenever they can. Guide you on your journey.*

Joy must be old—really, *really* old—to be a guardian, but their voice sounds just as young as mine. They sound like they're laughing as they speak. *I've been watching you closely, in both the world of the spirits and the world of the living. I know you well.*

The idea of anyone knowing me well sends a spark of hot coal plunging through me. If anyone knew me, they would see that I am too strange, too emotional, and not someone that can be loved. How can I be loved, if even my own mother doesn't love me because I'm so sad, and if my father didn't love me enough to stay, and if everyone in school always hates me, and if strangers from across the world hate me without even knowing my name? Shame is like a wild brush of thorns. I can't even look at my guardian.

Do you know what shame is? Joy asks me. *Yes, with your thoughts and head, I think you know what shame is. You could tell me the definition. But do you understand shame with your feeling and your emotion? When you are ashamed, it isn't because of something you've done. It's because you are ashamed of your own life. Your own existence. You want to apologize for living.*

Their words make sense. More sense than anything has in a long while. It's true, isn't it? I feel bad for who I am. Like I don't deserve to exist.

You deserve to exist. If you didn't deserve to exist, then you wouldn't exist. You don't need to feel bad for living, beloved child. I am so happy that you're alive.

"You might be the only one who is."

Even if no one else in the world loved you, you would still deserve to exist. But this simply isn't the case, Moon. There are people who love you, and don't even know you. People who will love you and haven't had the chance to meet you yet. And your mother. She loves you so very much.

"I've never met anyone who loves me. Only people who hate me."

The people who have shown you so much hatred have not discovered the love they need for themselves yet. They hate others in fear and in anger and in pain. Their pain causes you pain, too. How could they truly love themselves, wholly and fully, with peaceful understanding that they are worthy, and then attempt to take that worthiness from others? They're hurting, too, Moon.

It feels like Joy is just another voice trying to convince me that I should try being happy. Don't they know that I've tried being happy? I'd rather be happy than sad.

I don't mean to dismiss your pain. The pain you have felt is real. It's one that I have witnessed in many, for hundreds of thousands of lifetimes. You are not alone in this.

It feels like I am. This sadness is endless. What's the point of anything, when all I will feel is this black hole inside me, and the wish that my life will end?

There's nothing wrong with being sad. There are many in your world who would rather ignore pain. They decide it's easier to pretend that it isn't there, to force themselves to act like they are happy instead. But even if you look away from it, the pain will remain. It will only grow, the longer you try to ignore it. It's good that you see your pain. Now you must survive it. You must begin to heal it.

"But how do I do that?" I ask them.

There is an answer. You already know what it is. You already know what you must do.

I squint my eyes in confusion, but in that moment I can feel the beat of the truth inside me, so quickly that by the time that moment is over, I've already forgotten again.

Joy's leaves sparkle and dance. *But I can tell you what I hope for you, Moon. I hope you will see how worthy your life is—that you, too, deserve to exist, no matter what lies anyone says. I hope you will feel the power that is inside you. You are so powerful—powerful enough to receive hatred and turn it into love, if that's what you choose to do. I hope you feel with excitement the joy and love that awaits you, and how much you will appreciate your newfound happiness, the people who love and respect you, knowing the pain you have felt and survived. They're waiting for you, Moon. They will be so very happy when they meet you. I hope, so much, that you will find your peace.*

But I can feel dirt cracking and splintering beneath my feet, threatening to suck me in. I'm afraid I'll never find something like peace because I'm worried that something is wrong with me. Something has to be wrong with me, to always be in so much pain. To hurt so much that sometimes I'm worried I'll never feel happiness again.

Nothing is wrong with you, Moon. You exist in your world exactly as you were meant to exist. You will find that happiness. I have seen the many cycles of life. I have seen that every living human will always feel sadness, and pain—but they will feel joy as well.

My guardian stops speaking. I've been in the spirit realm for a while now, and didn't Dragon warn me? The longer I stay here, the more invisible I'll become in your world.

"Please," I say. "Tell me what I need to do in the world of the living. I'm turning invisible. I'm going to vanish completely if I don't do something."

Joy's voice is in my mind, but it feels even quieter than it had before. *A part of you still wants to be in the spirit world,* they tell me, *and so a part of you is still trapped here. You are afraid of the world of the living, more than you are afraid of these realms.*

But this isn't what I need to hear. These aren't the

detailed instructions I was expecting that would stop me from disappearing.

Love is its own power, Moon. It's an energy, too. Loving yourself can always give you the energy you need.

Joy sounds far away now. Just as abruptly as the star, when I blink, the tree in front of me is gone. The hill and the plains are, too.

"Moon!"

I spin around. Dragon sits up, rubbing their eyes. I look down and see that, to them, I'm a mirage of light fading back into sight. "I thought you'd vanished forever. You were gone for days. I wasn't sure what to do. What happened?"

There's so much to tell Dragon—about my guardian, and everything that they told me—but I realize why I left Joy so quickly. It's time. There's an alarm blaring in my head. Before I can even open my mouth to warn Dragon, or to tell them goodbye, I'm pulled *down*.

I'm in my bed.

The sun is rising outside my window.

I didn't even have a chance to speak to Dragon. I hope they'll come back to visit me again. I hope they won't stay there on that cliff, waiting for me to return.

I think about Joy, who has seen me from the time I was born and knows everything about me and has wished me happiness. They might even still be aware of me, even as I sit here in the world of the living.

When I hold up my hand, my heart sinks. It's still see-through—and not only that, but the invisibility is spreading down my arm, too.

At this rate, it'll only take a week before I'm completely gone.

What will happen then?

Will anyone notice I've disappeared?

Will anyone even remember that I'd ever been here?

CLOVE

It's hard to believe that, with everything happening—Wolf and Dragon and my guardian and the Keeper—I *still* have to go to school.

I stay in bed beneath the covers, and I give the best performance of my life, coughing and sneezing and groaning and all, but my mom takes my temperature and looks straight into my eyes and tells me I'm not sick, so I leave the house early enough in the morning that there's still a light chill in the breeze. I walk up the cracked sidewalk, through the empty roads and lines of brick apartment buildings that might as well be abandoned and very well could be, not a single other soul left in this city.

I'm lost in my own thoughts, my worries and fears, so it's some time before I look up at the sky. The sky is the light blue I'm used to seeing, but there are patterns, too, swirls of purple and orange and green, patterns that reflect in the light like waves of energy, strokes moving back and forth like the auroras.

The sky looks like it belongs in the spirit world.

I stop and stare, my heart pounding harder and harder the more I realize what I'm seeing. I'm awake, and I'm in the world of the living—so why am I seeing something that belongs in the higher realms?

I'd started to go invisible only a few days before. Joy said that a part of me still wants to be in the spirit world, but what if there's something else? I shouldn't have stayed in the spirit realm long enough to become completely solid. The star said there would be consequences. And now, here's all the proof I ever needed to see.

It's like the two worlds are colliding.

★

I'm the first one in the classroom, sitting in the pod of white walls and a white floor, at the single desk with my journal. I've been scribbling new lines in Blue's story every now and then with my invisible hand, but it's hard to concentrate now. There's a flurry of voices and laughter and suddenly the door slaps open and Lilah and

Wiley wander inside. I drop my pencil and put my hand in my hoodie pocket, where it'll have to stay hidden.

"The news says it's a rare atmospheric phenomenon," Lilah's saying.

"What, like a storm or something?"

"I don't know," Lilah says with a shrug. "What do you think, Moon? Did you see the sky this morning?"

I look up at them, my heart racing. This is the first time since I started crying on my first day of school that either of them has asked me a direct question. I've just been pretending not to exist since then, and they went along with me, but now . . .

Lilah stares at me for one long moment before she speaks. I'm worried that the more she looks at me, the more invisible I'll be. What if a whole patch of skin goes missing on my cheek? The invisibility has been spreading from my hand and down my arm, but who knows what the rules of turning invisible are?

"You're really quiet," she says. "Has anyone ever told you that?"

I pretend to stare at something I've written in my journal, though I haven't written anything on my new page yet.

"You don't have to be scared of anything," Lilah says. "I'm really nice. Well, I try to be, anyway. And Wiley is, too. This is our second year being podmates together. I think it's because we always give the same answers on that personality test. We also have a lot of the same interests. The people that were in our pod last year had the same interests, too, but we didn't get along as well."

She stops talking and stares at me with those big eyes, like she's waiting for me to say something, anything—but the longer she stares, the more I begin to feel a heat growing in my chest. There's just a blankness. I don't know what to say. And even if I did, Lilah and Wiley would probably just laugh at whatever words come out of my mouth anyway.

Was Joy right? I think they might have been. I think I really do feel ashamed of my own existence.

Wiley leans back in his chair, watching me. "I don't always like to talk, either," he says. "I hate when people think that, just because I'm quiet, I'm also shy. It's not a bad thing to be shy. But that's just not what I am. I don't always feel like talking because I don't always have anything to say. But then people get uncomfortable, and they decide being quiet means I'm shy, and they decide that's a bad thing. It can be a whole lot easier to just be alone sometimes."

Lilah frowns. "But isn't that what shy means?"

"No," Wiley says, "that's what being an *introvert* means. I'm an introvert. I get tired around a lot of other people really easily, and at the end of the day, I need to be by myself so I can watch TV or play video games or something. But just because I'm an introvert, doesn't mean I'm shy, too."

"Oh, I get that," Lilah says. "I think I might be shy."

"Yeah, right," Wiley says. "You're not shy."

"Please don't tell me what I am and what I'm not," Lilah says.

Wiley sighs. "Okay. I'm sorry. But why do you think you're shy?"

"Well, I do talk a lot," Lilah says, "and I don't get tired around other people. I guess that means I'm an extrovert. But I also get nervous around people when I'm meeting them for the first time."

"Oh, yeah," Wiley says. "I forgot how quiet you were last year when class began."

"I think it's okay to be shy," Lilah says, sitting up even straighter. "I think it's okay for all of us to be exactly who we are, even if it's different from other people."

I frown at the blank page in my journal. Joy said I deserve to exist. I try to remind myself of that. But my little voice, saying that I deserve to be here, is like a tiny shell against an ocean of people.

When I look up, Lilah and Wiley are staring at me with that same expression I'm so used to seeing—like maybe one of them said something to me, but I was so caught in my head that I didn't hear them speaking. I feel the shame returning like an old friend.

But I pause.

I decide to believe, even for a moment, that I deserve to exist. That I know there are people who also know my worth.

Lilah and Wiley's expressions don't change—but I think I know what Dragon meant when they said there's magic in the world of the living, too. With just that thought alone, I start to feel like a jewel encased in a solid stone—safe, protected, loved. It doesn't matter what Lilah and Wiley think of me or what their expressions say. It doesn't matter what they think, or how I feel, or how I react. I would still deserve love anyway.

The screen on the wall turns on and our teacher

comes into view. She says good morning, and that it's time to begin. She does roll call, and we can hear the tinny little voices of other classmates in other pods. I frown, looking at the seat Andrew usually takes. He's late, but the teacher doesn't seem to notice. She even skips right over his name, along with a few others.

I expect Lilah to say something, to raise her hand and say that Andrew is missing, but she doesn't say a word as she gets out her tablet along with Wiley as the class begins. It's still bothering me when I hear Wiley just a few minutes later.

"It's weird that they haven't given us four classmates like usual this year," he whispers. "I wonder why they choose only three."

Lilah nods, distracted. "It feels emptier than usual. Like something's missing."

I want to ask what they're talking about. There *are* four of us. Neither notice my confused stare.

"Maybe more kids are being homeschooled this year, so they didn't have enough for all the pods?" Lilah says.

"Andrew."

They both look at me, eyebrows high. This is the first time I've spoken to them.

My voice is hoarse, strained—but I force myself to keep going. "Andrew is the fourth classmate."

Isn't he?

Now they really look concerned. They stare at me, then look at each other. "Who is Andrew?" Lilah asks.

My heart feels weighted in my chest, so heavy that it can't beat. "Our fourth classmate," I say. "He was just here with us."

Lilah and Wiley look at each other again, like they think I've told a very unfunny joke and feel a little sorry for me. Before I can say anything else, the teacher asks us why we're talking when we're supposed to be doing silent reading, and both Lilah and Wiley return to bending their heads over their tablets.

Now *I'm* confused. He'd been here, *right here,* just sitting right beside me. Why can't Lilah and Wiley remember him?

Did I make Andrew up in my head, like Blue?

The spirit world is colliding with the world of the living, and I'm not the only one who has begun to disappear.

★

I run all the way home, gasping breaths tearing at my sides. The sky is turning darker even though it's still afternoon. It's purple, almost black now. People are out of their houses and apartments, when they're supposed to be inside, pointing up at the sky in awe.

I get back home and slam open the door, ready to close my eyes and go back to the spirit world—but I pause in the living room.

Ms. Stella isn't there.

Neither is my mom.

Usually, my mother's left some sort of note or a meal in the fridge or in a cold pot on the stove before she gets ready for work. I don't see anything—no food, no note, no sign that she'd even been in the apartment.

"Mom?" I say. "Mom!"

She doesn't answer me. The spirit world is coming into the world of the living, and now my mom has vanished, too.

Tears start to sting my eyes, and they only stop when I hear footsteps. I run, following the sound, hope rising in my chest like a feather on the breeze. I turn the corner in time to see my mom coming out of her bedroom, adjusting her nursing outfit.

"Moon?" she says, looking at my face, my tears. "What's wrong? What happened?"

I'm crying so hard that I can't find a way to get the words out of my mouth. She pulls me into a hug and smooths down my hair. I can't remember the last time my mom held me like this. She hugged me when I was younger all the time. What happened? What changed?

She pulls away, wiping the tears from my face with her thumbs. "Can't you say what happened?" she asks.

But I don't know where to start, even if I wanted to speak.

My mom sighs as she puts a hand to my cheek. She's used to my silence, my tears, and she's already given up—or maybe she just doesn't know what to say. Maybe she's just as afraid. "I'm sorry, honey," she says. "But I have to go. I'm already running late for my shift."

My heart sinks in my chest as she stands and walks away, hurrying into the kitchen with her purse over her shoulder and her keys in her hand. "Maybe I should schedule another counseling appointment. You can try again, to talk about what's bothering you then."

ELDERBERRY

Ms. Stella walks into the apartment a couple of hours after my mom leaves and greets me with a smile. She's quiet. It's surprising because I got used to her filling up the silence with her stories—but today, she watches me like she can feel words trying to make their way out of my mouth. I wear a hoodie, hiding my hands in my pockets, just like I did all day at school. I stare at her while she stares at me.

I ask, "Why aren't you speaking?"

She doesn't celebrate that I've used my voice, which I'm grateful for, because I don't think it's something that needs to be celebrated. She only looks at me as if I've been talking with her all along, all this time, who cares, nothing new that I've used my mouth. She gives the smallest shrug. Maybe she doesn't know the answer to that question herself. "Would you like me to speak?"

I think I would like her to. There's something about her words that are soothing, that enter my chest and my heart and let me know that I'm going to be all right. No matter how I'm feeling today or will feel the next, something about her words tell me I am loved.

Ms. Stella is still sitting there watching me, patiently, like she doesn't mind my silence, like she can see the colors that've started to swirl in my head, the waves of purple and blue and green, black holes and an infinite number of universes inside me. "Yes," I tell her. "Please."

She decides that, today, she will tell me a story. "There was once a child who was born with wings. They lived in a village, in an imaginary town. The villagers did not like this child very much. They were afraid. *Wings belong on birds, not humans,* they said. They told this child that they were a monster, and the child began to believe them. They had so much shame for their wings. They prayed every night that when they woke again, they'd no longer have feathers growing from their back so that they would be loved by the other villagers. But no prayer ever helped. They tried to hide the wings beneath their clothes, even if it meant they would become bent and cramped, but the villagers could still see the outline, the hump of the hidden wings. The child hated their wings so much that one day, they sat down and tried to pluck each and every feather out. It hurt so much; but even then, the villagers saw what the child did. The village elder told the child it didn't matter if they still had wings or not. *You will forever be a monster, for the simple fact that you were born that way.* Oh, how the child cried. They decided there wasn't any point to life. They would never be loved. They would never be accepted. They decided that they wanted to die. They walked to the cliff at the edge of the village, but before they jumped, the child thought to themself—*before I die, maybe I will try to use my wings, just this once.* They decided they would try to fly. They let their wings break free from their clothes, and they focused hard, as hard as they could. They closed their eyes and they flapped and flapped and flapped, and they lifted from the ground and flew straight up into the air. They saw the most beautiful sights: the bluest sky and the pinkest clouds, a world far beyond the village that they had never seen before. And there, right there in the sky, they saw for the first time other beings. They were humans, and they all had wings, too. These beings were so excited to see the child. They welcomed the child with so much joy. These beings knew the child was not a monster, knew that they were special and that they belonged. Finally, the child began to believe they were worthy of love." Ms. Stella smiles. "If you had wings, would you want to fly?"

"No," I tell her. "I'm too afraid of heights."

She laughs. "I think I would like to fly. There's so much to be seen."

Ms. Stella watches and waits like she always does.

"But what does the story mean?" I ask her.

"What do you think it means?"

The child reminds me so much of myself. The way they'd been convinced to believe that they were a monster by everyone around them, the way they hated themself because they were different.

"When we're born," Ms. Stella says, "our souls are planted in these bodies, and the world hasn't had a chance to show us any harm yet. We only know love because that is what we are—love, unconditionally, for ourselves and for others. And then the years begin to pass, and then we begin to see that some people are treated differently, even though our souls are all the same. We start to believe that we are not enough when we don't receive the love we are worthy of; we begin to feel ashamed of ourselves, of our existence. Some people take this shame out on others. They need to think they are better, stronger, smarter to fill the hole of hurt because they have forgotten that they are made of unconditional love. They think that if they are better than another person, they will believe they are worthy of love, too. If they realized they are made of love, then they would see others around them and know that they are made of unconditional love as well—that no one person is ever worth more than another, or ever any less.

"And there are some whose shame hurts themselves. They start to believe the hatred that they are shown and think that they aren't worthy of love. I know this is hard, Moon; but I also believe that you are able to learn that you are worthy of love, no matter how others treat you. You are worthy of love, no matter what others think of you. What a courageous soul you have, Moon, to want to learn a lesson like this. To learn how to love yourself."

I shake my head. "But how?" I ask her. "How do I

learn to love myself?" Even if this is the answer, it isn't so easy to do.

"Isn't that always the question?"

She stands, abruptly, as usual. The hour is already up, and Ms. Stella leaves me with only a smile.

VALERIAN

I sit and try to leave my body, struggling not to cry in frustration. I haven't rested at all. It's almost morning, and I sat up all night. I haven't been able to concentrate enough to jump out of my body again. Dragon isn't here to help me this time. What if I can never go back without their help?

And then I hear it.

I hear the hollow, wailing cries.

For a second, I'm not sure if I've just imagined the sounds. Maybe I fell asleep without realizing it and the cries were in my nightmares, the echo still vibrating in my lungs. I can see through the window that the sun is rising to an orange and pink sky, waves of energy and light sparkling in the clouds. There are the soft peeps of birds waking up, and in a few minutes, I'm sure that my mom will come into my room and tell me it's time to get ready for the day.

But there—beneath it all, muffled like it's beneath water, I can hear the sound.

It's the same wailing cries I'd heard in the spirit world. The sound of the monster that follows me everywhere I go.

My throat is dry when I swallow. I climb out of bed and crawl across the floor, my breath trapped in my lungs, too scared to come out and face whatever it is I'm about to see. I lean up to my window to look outside.

And there—towering over the skyline of apartment buildings and towers, I see the black haze. The hollow cry comes again, even louder. Birds fly into the air and surround the monster like gnats. It pauses. It straightens, standing tall over the buildings.

And it turns to look right at me.

I duck beneath my window before the monster can see me, and before I can see it clearly, behind its cloak of smoke and ash. I'm shivering with fear. The fear slows my pulse, my body, my head. Another vibrating, sorrowful sound echoes. I think that this time, it might have said my name. *Moon.*

I throw myself back into my bed and hide beneath

my sheets. *It's just a dream,* I tell myself, again and again. *It's just a dream.*

The monster can't be real.

It should never have been able to leave the spirit world.

There's no way it can really be here.

I lie still, curled up beneath my blanket, waiting to feel a shadow over me—but the longer I wait, the more minutes tick by, the more I realize that the monster hasn't come for me. Not yet. I look out my window again, and it's disappeared completely.

Everyone had the ability to do magic in each and every world, though not everyone chose to. The Magician taught Blue how to cloak herself in invisibility and how to float up into the air until she was as tall as the tallest tree. The Magician taught Blue how to make potions and how to sing noisy frogs to sleep and even how to walk between worlds, from her own world and into yours.

Magic wasn't always easy to learn. Blue would start to cry some nights, bent over leather-bound books and texts with small scribbles of writing that taught the secrets of magicians who took forms in many different worlds. You see, the spirit world is not only a place of spirits from your world. There are an infinite number of worlds, yes—and the spirits of each world come together on the other side of the veil.

Blue kept trying her very best. She was intent on becoming the best magician that had ever lived. She believed that if she studied magic hard enough, she might just be able to find a way to go back to the sky again.

The Magician had taught Blue all the magic they knew, but they were hurt by Blue, too. They remembered the words Blue had said in the garden many months before. They knew that their daughter, their child, didn't want to live in this world anymore.

It was on the anniversary of this day that Blue told the Magician why it was she seemed so sad all the time, no matter what the Magician did to make her happy. "I'm meant to be in the sky," she said. "I'm supposed to be a star—shining greater than anyone. When I shine like the stars above, I know that I am worthy of love. Even if the stars abandoned me in this world—if I can shine like them, I will show them. They will see. I'm just as great as they'll ever be."

This hurt the Magician very much, because they loved Blue with all their heart, and had spent many years raising Blue to be the fine young person that she was. "But why would you want to leave me behind?" they asked. "Aren't you happy here, with me?"

Blue loved the Magician, but the truth was that she wasn't happy. She wasn't sure if she ever would be, knowing that the star had left her here—kicked her out of the sky as if she didn't belong. There was always a sadness that cloaked her like a shadow.

ROSE

My mom sees the circles of purple beneath my eyes and decides this is enough of a reason to stay home today. I sit with my journal in my bed. I have to figure out how to get back to the spirit realm again. I need to help Wolf and Dragon and all the beings—save them from the Keeper. I have to stop the worlds from colliding, stop myself from turning invisible. I've kept my hand out of view from my mom, and I always wear a hoodie in front of her now, even when I'm hiding beneath my covers, but my entire arm is see-through now, and the skin around my neck and my stomach is starting to fade away. How much time do I have left before I completely disappear?

It's like I can't leave on my own because I can't concentrate. I'm too tired. I don't have enough energy . . .

Energy. Didn't Joy tell me something about energy?

They said that loving myself can always give me the energy I need.

Loving myself feels impossible, when I hate myself so much. I feel ashamed even trying to think the words in my head. *I love myself.*

But it might just be the only way I can get back to the spirit realm again. I try to sit and close my eyes again. I try to think the words. *I love myself. I love me.* It feels like a lie, but another thought comes to me instead. *I might not love myself yet, but I think I can learn to. With time, I will learn to love myself. And that's good enough because I deserve love.*

I feel a jolt.

★

The storm above roils, multiple tornadoes threatening to funnel through the air. The pyramid has streaks of black mold, the faint glow dimmed. The city's other buildings are gone. There are only spines of buildings now, vines of thorns that snake along the old streets, wrapping around the beings. Wolf is still asleep, his breaths low. His fur is intertwined with vines of thorns, brown and wilting rose petals, as if he's become a garden. He doesn't wake up, not when I put a hand on his nose or in the fur of his scruff. I lie down against him. Maybe I'd already decided, before I left, that I would come here to lie beside Wolf for all the rest of time.

But I see something move in the corner of my eye. My heart jumps. A shadowed figure runs across the road, toward the drawbridge.

"Dragon!" I call, but even as their name leaves my mouth, I realize it isn't them.

The hunched figure has on a cloak that hides their face. They glance over their shoulder at me for a split second, and then turn back around and run. I almost slip trying to follow, racing forward to catch up to them as they hobble away.

I run and slide in front of them, forcing them to stop before they can step into the pyramid's entrance.

The cloaked figure is very short, shorter than even me. Their face is hidden completely in shadow, but I can hear their exasperation in their voice alone. "Who are you?" they demand. "Why are you chasing me?"

My breath is heavy. It takes me a second to catch it.

"My name is Moon," I say. "And I need help. I'm looking for someone named Dragon."

The being is incredulous. "No one is here. No one has lived here for thousands of years."

"Not even the Keeper?"

The figure stiffens. Even without being able to see their face clearly, I can feel their frown. "She'd once been known as the Keeper," the being says, "but she's changed. There's a Shadow that has melded with her. She is now only known as the Monster."

My heart falls. It's because of me. It's all because I helped her when I shouldn't have.

The being tries to hobble around me, continuing on the path. Suspicion rises. Why do I have the feeling that they're hiding something?

"Isn't the pyramid abandoned?" I ask them.

"Exactly," they say. "So it might as well be mine, right?"

"Wait," I say, hurrying to walk beside them before they reach the entrance. "Do you know where the Monster has gone?" I ask them.

The person points up, so I look up, too. The rumbling clouds, the storm in the sky. Dragon had been right. The storm really is alive. "She's the storm?"

"Not quite." But the being doesn't seem willing to explain much more.

If the Keeper—the *Monster*—is in the sky, then she could see me. She could be watching me right now, and she could appear from the clouds, attack, and imprison me and this stranger.

The being pushes past me. "What are you doing here, anyway? You are a human child. You should hurry back along to the world of the living."

"I can't. Not until I find my guardian. I need to find them so that I can defeat the Monster and save myself—no, save everyone, in both the world of the living and the spirit realm."

The cloaked figure watches me from the shadows for a moment, then shrugs. "Good luck." They step into the pyramid's entrance.

I stand there for some time. A mist begins to move across the plains. I take a deep breath, and I step into the pyramid, too.

The white lights are still on, but it's eerie inside the pyramid now. There are roots that grow down the walls, and so much dust drifts through the air that it's like a haze. I sneeze over and over again, my eyes watering. Even though I'd stepped in right after the stranger, they've already disappeared. I walk down one hall, and then the next. The Keeper had never taken me down this path before. The hall is filled with doors, one right after the other—but they're all different. One is pink and has a golden knocker. The other is a bright blue and looks more like a force field. Another is metal and looks like it would take ten people to yank it open.

A voice echoes as if on a loudspeaker. *Why, pray tell, are you following me?*

"You never told me who you are," I say.

A door with faded green paint slams open. "And why is that any of your business?"

If they know something that could help me defeat the Keeper and save everyone, then I need to figure out their secret. I narrow my eyes. "I told you who I was, didn't I?"

They sigh dramatically. "Fine. If I tell you, will you leave me alone?"

"Yes."

"You'll promise to never bother me, not ever again?"

"Yes, I promise."

The figure pulls back their cloak. They are much older than I was expecting, with lines across their face like they're over one hundred years old. They have a bald head and a large green beard. It takes me a moment to realize that it's vines and leaves and flowers that grow from this person's chin, and not hair. What's most surprising of all? They look so familiar. They feel like someone I've known a thousand lifetimes before, like a close friend whose name I've just forgotten.

They don't notice. They mumble and mutter and sigh about being pulled into other beings' adventures that are a waste of time.

"What's your name?" I ask them, voice quiet.

The person gives a bemused smile. "Well, I have lived so long that I've forgotten it myself, but my friends know me as the Magician."

I feel warmth spread throughout me at the word alone. "The Keeper said that she's a magician, too."

"Yes, well, she was right. We're all magicians. We all have magic, power, inside us. But there are some who become warped by their pain. They use their pain as an excuse to hurt others."

"The Keeper has been hurt?"

"Yes, of course," the Magician says. "Haven't we all been hurt at some point in our lives? Especially as children! Goodness me, I think that's when we all experience the most pain we ever will, because we're just so *surprised*, wouldn't you say? We're not expecting people to want to hurt or harm us or tell us that we aren't enough to be loved. Love is all we'd ever known, so it comes as a bit of a shock when people hurt us."

I think I understand what they mean. It's always a little surprising, isn't it? Even when I think I've come to expect it, there's still a part of me that wonders why anyone would want to harm another person.

The Magician goes on. "There is an ability to take that pain, to heal from it, to grow and learn from it—that is magic, this transformation. That is true power. There are others, though, like the Keeper, who use their power to take their pain and transfer it to others. They allow the hurt to spread. It's like a parasite. Nasty business."

I begin to wonder what it is that hurt the Keeper in her lifetime. Before she came to the spirit world, she must have felt so much pain to want to hurt so many souls. But that's not an excuse, is it? She made these choices.

"I can't have pity for her," I tell the Magician. "Not

when she's hurt me, and Wolf, and Dragon, and so many others, too."

"You don't need to have pity for anyone," the Magician says. "You don't even need to forgive, and you certainly don't need to forget what she has done. But sometimes forgiveness can be more about yourself, and the power you refuse to give to her with your anger. Forgiveness is its own magic. It's quite transformative, too. Besides," the Magician says, "haven't we also hurt others, in the end? Even when we haven't meant to."

And at this mention, a familiar shame burns through me. Because it's true. I chose to help the Keeper. Because I agreed to take light from the star, the Keeper was able to hurt so many others. She put everyone under her spell and destroyed this city. Because of me.

"Even more powerful than anything else," the Magician says, gaze watchful, "is the power to forgive yourself. Knowing you're still worthy of love, no matter what you've done. You can decide to forgive yourself, and do what you can to fix those mistakes."

The Magician is still so familiar that I can't look away from them. "I think I might have already known you," I say. They raise a skeptical eyebrow. "I've been writing a story about a magician," I tell them, "and a child named Blue."

"Well, that doesn't surprise me at all," the Magician says. "The spirit world and the world of the living are so very closely connected. Your imagination comes from the land of the spirits. It is often how we communicate with you. We like to send you messages through your dreams and your stories. If I am a character in your tale, then maybe there is someone on this side who is also this child named Blue."

I frown in confusion. "Were you trying to send me a message?"

"Oh, no, little human," the Magician laughs. "I have no idea who you are."

They turn their back on me with a sigh and the twirl of a hand. "Well," they say, "good luck. If you need my assistance, you know where to find me. But something tells me you know exactly what to do."

ASTER

The whispers chant my name, and when I close my eyes, the gate in my mind opens.

The sand around me holds the patterns of the wind, lines carving through the grains. It stretches for miles, past the horizon. It looks like a desert, but without the sun, the sand holds bits of blue ice. I shiver, steam rising from my mouth as I take a breath. Above me, the sky yawns open to the universe and its infinite number of stars, the sky so clear that I can even see the edges of other universes alongside ours, where I know there is an infinite number of children named Moon, maybe all of us, at this very moment, looking at the sky and thinking of one another with a small smile.

In front of me, just a few paces away, there is a single rock. It's as tall as I am, and it stands with patterns designed into its surface. It's not what an average rock would look like. Instead, it's perfectly smooth and round like a miniature globe, and it shines silver light. It looks like the moon. Well, not the moon that I know. It might just be the spirit of the moon from yet another world.

You have come a far way, Moon, my guardian says. *My name is Wisdom.*

I force myself to walk closer. "Hello."

I already know why you are here. I've known why you would come long before you were born, before your life was created in the light of a star; still, I want to hear your words.

I try not to shake as I tell them the story of everything that has happened: that I helped the Keeper, and that because of this mistake, the spirit realm is destroyed, beings forced into sleep for all of eternity. I'm now starting to disappear in the world of the living, and some people have already disappeared completely. The Shadow monster has followed me, even there. I tell them about Wolf and Dragon, and how I need to save everyone that I love from the Keeper, who is now the Monster.

By the time I've finished, I'm exhausted and out of breath, and I feel my eyes burning with tears.

Take a moment, Wisdom says. *Let yourself cry if this*

is what you wish. Let yourself breathe. Let yourself exist.

I don't want to let myself cry. Not at first. There are so many people in the world of the living who believe that crying is weak. I never wanted to cry in front of anyone who laughed at me. I didn't want them to know how hurt I really was. Crying makes me feel ashamed. It's always felt like admitting defeat.

But now, Wisdom waits with patient silence, the sort of patience that can belong only to someone or something that has seen the beginning of time itself, that has seen the uncomprehending before existence. And the tears come. I don't know how long I stand there, salt on my cheeks. I feel impatient to get the help I need, but the more I cry, the more the tears come, and I realize how much I had been holding back—how many emotions have been stored inside me for so long. The cries begin to shake my body, and sobs control my shoulders and my chest. And even when those slow so that only tears drip from my chin, Wisdom still waits.

Why haven't you let yourself cry, little Moon? Wisdom asks when I can breathe again.

"I can't cry," I tell them. "Even when I've tried, the emotions disappear, and I don't feel anything at all. I only become tired." So tired that I have to close my eyes, so tired that I wonder why I'm still alive. "Is something wrong with me?"

Nothing. Nothing is wrong with you, nothing at all. You are perfection. You were created from the threads of this universe, from the light of stars. If something is wrong with you, then something is wrong with the sun, and something is wrong with the moon, and something is wrong with planets and galaxies and life and love. You are who you were meant to be, and who you are meant to become. And when your time on this earth ends, as it must, you will be granted the wisdom to look upon your life. You will be so proud of yourself, child.

I know the answer to all my questions, deep inside me, even as I have so many lessons to learn still. I think of other souls. My mother, Ms. Stella and Mr. Richmond, Lilah and Wiley and Andrew, the children who have shown me so much hatred, the strangers who don't want me to exist: every single being that is still in the world of the living. They all have their own lessons to learn, too.

"What do I need to do?" I ask Wisdom.

There is only one way you will be able to defeat the being you call the Monster, and to save the lost souls—to stay alive in the world of the living, and not be trapped here in the spirit world. You must have hope.

I can feel the frustration bubbling up. This is what adults always say, but I don't know how to feel hope. I don't know if there's any point to hope. How can there be a point to any of this—to any of the pain, the suffering—when it's all going to end anyway?

But I can feel Wisdom's steadfast gaze.

Your life as Moon will eventually end, yes, they say. *But the point is not the end of your life, but the life you live along the way. The hope is in the chance for joy that you have not experienced, and that you will experience soon. The hope is in the friends you have not yet made. The hope is in your life, Moon, and all the possibility for growth and change that exists still. I know it's hard where you are, and when you are, and I'm sorry. I'm so sorry for the pain you feel. But that will not be your entire life. You've lived twelve years of sadness. Imagine what it'll be like when you live twelve years of joy, and so much more.*

"I can't be happy always, all the time."

Maybe not. But you can't be sad always, either. Sadness is a cycle. It will always come to an end. Wouldn't you like to see what happens next?

Even though a part of me, an old part that I know

too well, only wants to argue, I can't hide the curiosity from myself. It's true that I wonder what my life will be like. Will I stay in the city, in my bedroom with my four white walls, or will I travel the world? Will I study writing, and publish a book? Wisdom said I might even make friends one day—friends who understand me, who don't go by he or she; friends who enjoy speaking with me, who realize that I'm smart and funny and kind, who also have hidden wings. There's so much in the world of the living that I haven't experienced yet.

I ask Wisdom, "What do I need to do to stop the Monster?"

I do not have that answer, Wisdom says. Disappointment slides through me. *You need to find your third guardian. They will help you find your way.*

But when I try to close my eyes and listen to hear them whispering my name, there's only silence. "I can't hear their call."

Wisdom doesn't respond. I feel the truth: They have told me all I need to know, and though they will always be here for me, they won't speak here and now anymore. The answers are already inside me. I have to trust myself now.

PROTEA

When I open my eyes, I find that the Magician is sitting in the hall, bubbles all colors of the rainbow growing through the air around them. They wave a hand at the bubbles so that they pop, and they stand up, dusting off the backs of their legs.

"You stayed," I say, surprise in my voice.

They seem embarrassed. "I'll admit, I got a little worried when a few days passed and there was no sign of you."

I think the Magician might just be the kind of person who secretly cares, even when they don't want anyone to know. They walk with me out of the halls and through the pyramid and across the bridge, back to where a sleeping Wolf still waits, flowers growing around his teeth. I put a hand on his snout. It hurts to leave him here like this.

"You are rather brave, I must say," the Magician says. "I don't think I have ever quite seen a human child like you before."

I lift my hand from Wolf's fur. "I don't feel so brave. I'm always scared."

"Yes, well. Isn't that where courage lives? That space between fear and doing something that scares you anyway."

I know it's time to go—that any second now, I'll be pulled back down to your world—but before I can even take another breath, there's a sudden burst of wind. There isn't any warning. A gust so strong that it blows ash and dust into the air, swirling around like a small tornado that lives and dies within seconds. I'm knocked off my feet, thrown back to the dirt again, little rocks pinching my skin. A darkened cloud rolls across the sky, blocking out any possibility of light.

The Magician strains against the wind, squinting their eyes. "It's her," they shout over the storm. "You have to go. Leave—now!"

I try to squeeze my eyes shut, whispering to myself that it's time to go back to your world again. But I hear her laugh, and I know I can't leave the spirit realm now, not when a part of me wants so badly to stay behind. Not when I want to make sure that Wolf will be all right. I have to face her. I have to force her to release Wolf from this spell—to give him back to me and save all the other beings.

And when I open my eyes, there she is—standing before me and the Magician.

The Monster still looks so much like she had in her original form, but she's taller now, her limbs and neck stretched, her skin a sickly pale white. The butterflies that had once flitted about her strands of hair are worms and maggots. A dark cloud surrounds her, twisting around her body like a spiraling snake of smoke. It looks so much like the Shadow that followed me every time I came to this realm.

She gives me a sharp smile. "Hello, little Moon," she says. "It's so good to see you. How long has it been?"

I'd been so distracted by the sight of the Monster that I hadn't noticed Dragon standing beside her. Dragon's eyes shine with fear. The Monster pushes Dragon forward with another gust of wind, and they fall into the dirt.

"You have always struck me as particularly brave,"

the Monster says as she walks closer to me. The ground smolders beneath her feet with every step. She's barefoot, her feet like talons.

I run forward to help Dragon up. "What're you doing here?" they whisper. "You shouldn't have come back!"

"Is that your friend?" the Monster asks, smile glimmering. "How sweet! I found them wandering the realm. I thought it was curious that someone had escaped my spell, so I decided to keep them as my pet. But the child is so troublesome." She sighs. "Always whining and asking that I turn the realm back to normal again."

Her gaze slides onto the Magician, like she'd known they were here all along but decided not to acknowledge them until now. I get the distinct feeling that they already know each other, the way her eyes narrow into an angry glare. I don't think I've ever seen so much hatred and rage on a face before.

"And what're you doing here?" the Monster asks.

"Waiting for you," the Magician says. "As usual."

"You don't belong here," she says. "You're supposed to be in the higher realms."

The higher realms? I've only been to the higher

realms three times now—when I met the star, Joy, and Wisdom. But I get the sense that any being who is supposed to be in the higher realms is a lot like them: powerful, old, and wise. The sort of being that's a guardian. I was right. The Magician was keeping a secret after all. Are they my guardian? Have they secretly been here to help me all along?

"You don't have to continue doing this," the Magician says to the Monster. "You can always stop. Change your ways. It's never too late."

The Monster smiles. "You should be proud! I'm as powerful as I am now because of you."

Dragon whispers beside me as they stand up. "You should leave. You should go back to the world of the living, Moon."

"I'm not leaving you."

The Magician's voice is low as they speak to the Monster. "That's one thing you never quite understood. I taught you tricks, but your power doesn't come from me, or anyone else. You haven't found that true power yet."

Her laugh is a screeching pierce. "I haven't found that power?" she repeats. Her wicked grin vanishes in an instant. "Look around you! If this is not power, then what is?"

"This isn't power," the Magician says calmly. "This is destruction. The more that you define your power by the pain of others, the less true power you have."

"You've always spewed pretty words, but it won't matter much, will it? When I'm finally rid of you, it won't matter at all."

The Magician doesn't seem afraid. They raise their chin. "That true power comes from you. Your true power is deep inside you. But you've blocked yourself from that power. Your fear blocks you."

The Monster's skin seems to vibrate with rage. "Afraid?" she says, her voice angry and low. "Of *what*?"

"That's the question I always wanted you to ask yourself," the Magician says. "You didn't want to look. You didn't want to see."

There's silence. Dust blows in waves around the Monster. Dragon whispers to me, "Maybe we should try to run while she's distracted."

"Run where? She'll only catch us." I wish I could tell Dragon to come with me to the world of the living, but I know they wouldn't be able to stay there forever. It wouldn't be fair to them. And what about Wolf and the Magician?

Well, maybe I don't need to worry about the Magician as much as I thought. In a split second, they hold up a palm, whispering words I can't hear. There's a blaze of white light that shines around me and Dragon, like a bubble of protection. The Magician turns their palm to the Monster, mumbling the beginning of another spell, but the Monster holds up both her hands and clenches them together, and the Magician is thrown through the air, soaring out of sight. I gasp and spin back around, and the Monster has appeared in front of me.

The Monster pops the bubble with her finger. She uses one long nail to raise my chin. "It's brave of you, child, to come here again."

I yank away. My voice is shaking, but I force myself to speak. "I never should've helped you. I didn't know you were going to hurt everyone like this."

She tilts her head to the side with a smile. "Didn't you?" she asks. "You must've had some sort of inkling."

My throat clenches. Wolf tried to warn me, and so did the star. I didn't listen to them.

"I think it's more likely," she continues, walking

closer to me as I back away slowly, "that you just didn't care. You wanted your freedom to stay here in the spirit realms, even if it meant other beings would have to suffer for it."

"That isn't true!" I yell. "I didn't know that you were going to—"

"It doesn't matter, little Moon. You think that I'm a monster?" she asks, grin widening. Her teeth are like needles. "What would that make you?"

Dragon's voice is hoarse. "Don't listen to her, Moon."

I feel tears rising. Wisdom said there was no shame in tears. I try to take a steady breath. "Release everyone," I tell her. "Let them go. Let Wolf wake up. They don't deserve this."

Her voice is suddenly high and shrill. It reminds me of the Shadow's scream, when it used to follow me everywhere. I clap my hands over my ears. "Do you think anyone deserves to be hurt? What about me?" she wails. "Do you think I deserved to be hurt, too?"

The Magician reappears at her side, palms up, eyes focused with determination. They open their mouth to begin another spell. The Monster sighs loudly, impatiently, and she spins. She grasps the Magician by their cheeks, pulling them up, up—off the ground, off their feet. They grasp the Monster's arm, but it's like iron—she doesn't budge.

"Let them go!" I scream.

The Monster ignores me. "Why do you insist on coming here?" she demands. "You know that I'll only force you to leave again and again."

The Magician's words are muffled. "I want to help you. I only want to help you."

My heart sinks. I should have realized that I'm not the only being in the universe with a guardian.

The Monster's mouth widens as if she plans to take a bite.

The Magician struggles for a moment, but only one.

Their skin begins to glow bright.

Hot-white and blue energy dances from them in waves. The Monster hisses and yanks her hand away, as if burned. She glares at the Magician, who floats away from her hands. The Magician looks at me, apologetic. They glow brighter, brighter, until I have to shield my eyes. There's a burst of light, and like a rocket or a shooting star, they fly into the sky, disappearing through the clouds. The Magician is a being in the higher realms. Even if they try to return immediately to help me fight the Monster again, it'll have been a few hours.

The Monster has already moved on. I feel tears growing in me, right along with my fury as I look away from the sky and back to her.

"I didn't appreciate the way you left me in my manor," she tells me. "You didn't say goodbye. Not even a thank-you."

I have to hide my fear. I can't let her see. "Let go of my friends."

"Your friends? Oh," she says with a laugh, "you mean this beast and this pathetic creature." I meet Dragon's eye. "I won't release them. They're both mine to do with as I please. They've lost their battles against me. You have, too."

"I haven't lost against you."

"No?" She tilts her head to the side. "Haven't you already realized the truth? You've learned that you're nothing without your guides. You're a sad, pitiful child with no purpose, and no one who loves you. Why, you can't even learn to love yourself because you know it's true. There's no one alive on Earth who would ever love you."

I know that Wolf would say she's wrong, but he's unmoving, so still that he's barely breathing. Dragon shakes their head. I can practically hear their thoughts bounce around in my head. *Please, Moon. Don't listen to her.*

"You might as well stay here, with me," the Monster says. "You can replace this creature as my pet. They're annoying, but you seem much quieter. You can travel the spirit realms and see glorious sights. Isn't this preferable to living out the rest of your life in misery?"

I'm shaking more than I ever had before.

When the alarm begins to blare, I barely even notice.

Wisdom had told me to have hope, but now, listening to the Monster, I don't know what to believe anymore.

It's true, isn't it? I've never known any sort of happiness before.

The alarm is getting louder now.

I'm frozen in ice, words stolen from my mind.

I could tell the Monster, couldn't I? Ask her to

keep me here longer, so that the golden chain wouldn't force me back into my body.

Dragon suddenly runs in between me and the Monster. "Run, Moon!" they scream. They raise their arms to the sky, and there's a flash of light, so bright that I have to squeeze shut my eyes.

WATER LILY

The world of the living is beneath the sea.

There's little light that can shine through the ocean's waves as bubbles float past me.

It's difficult to walk beneath water.

I'm weighted down as I try to jump forward with every step.

I was in the spirit realm for too much time.

I've completely vanished.

I was too late, and now there's nothing that I can do to save myself.

★

This is what depression feels like: to be trapped underwater, drowning, but desperately trying to swim for the surface. Hoping that when you reach out a hand, someone will pull you out again. I don't know what to do, but

I know that I can't just stay in my room, pinned beneath the weight of an ocean.

I spend the day wandering the city. The ocean gets darker as the day goes on. Every now and then, I see another person who is still in the world of the living. They walk around with ease, talking and laughing. No bubbles are released from their noses or their mouths. Their voices are muffled and cloudy underwater.

I reach the train station, and I climb the steps to the platform and sit on a bench, my hair floating around me like a halo. The train comes, and I swim in through the open doors. I find an empty seat and watch the brick buildings that pass in the windows. I think I see the black haze of a monster, but we move too fast, and by the time I've blinked, the smoke is gone.

The train makes one stop and then another. I swim back out open doors, floating among the few passengers that wait. Outside in the city streets, people seem unaware that they are underwater as they walk past me. I float into a coffee shop and watch someone who sits with their earbuds in, bubbles surrounding them.

When I return home, I slip through the glass front

doors and swim up the stairs. I hesitate outside the apartment. I can hear my mom on the other side. It's afternoon now. She's singing, probably happier without me and my sadness, which always seems to bring a shadow whenever I'm around.

Does she even remember that I ever existed?

I've vanished from this world and from everyone's memory, and she's living the life she would have if she didn't need to worry about the sad child named Moon.

I float in through the door. My mom is doing the dishes in the kitchen. She finishes up and dries her hands with a sigh, then sits down on the sofa, staring into space for a while.

She laughs at something, I don't know what. Probably just a passing thought.

Then she says, "I know you're there."

My heart would pound in my chest with fear if I still had one.

I forgot that my mom can speak to spirits, even if she can't see them.

She must think I'm a little spirit child, here in the world of the living when I shouldn't be.

(Is it true? Is that what I am?)

"I don't know what you want," she says, "but I probably won't be able to help you. It's best, I think, if you move on instead."

I just want to speak to her. I want to tell her how much I'm hurting, and how much it hurt, too, that she was so angry with me when I told her the truth that I didn't want to be alive anymore. I wish she hadn't put me into therapy because she was too afraid to look at my feelings, like she hoped it would cure my depression, instead of trying to talk to me. There's so much to say, and I can't say any of it now. I have never cried underwater before. My eyes sting from the extra salt, and I can feel myself fading even more.

Maybe, eventually, I will completely fade away, and I won't even remember myself.

"I can sense that you're young," my mom says. "I think that you should try to find your family. They must miss you. They'll be speaking to you even now, I bet— trying to let you know how much they love you, and how sorry they are that you have passed on."

She pauses for one long moment, for such a long, inhaled breath that I want to see her face. I swim around the sofa and stand in front of her, watch as her eyes slowly shut, forehead wrinkled and brows tugging together.

"I have a baby, too, you know."

My mom shouldn't be able to remember me.

I've vanished. I'm gone from this world.

"It's strange, but I'm only now realizing it—yes, I have a child. How could I have forgotten that? I love them so, so much. Their name is Moon."

She tilts her head to the side a little, still with a small frown. "I don't always know how to talk to them. I wish I could tell them how much they mean to me. They are my sun, my galaxy, my universe. I love them, and I'm so afraid for them sometimes—so scared I don't know what words to say to help them survive. Maybe I should say that I love them. Maybe that would be enough."

My mom's words warm my skin. I want to wave my arms around, scream that it's me, and that I'm here, but only bubbles leave my mouth.

My mom squints her eyes open, lost in thought. "It's funny," she says. "I'm starting to remember the days when I was a child now. I was an only child, like Moon, and my mom was a single mother, too. She loved me, of course she did—she loved me so much. But she had to work for us to live. She was always working, always so tired after she came home from her two, three, sometimes four jobs. She didn't have the energy to speak to me, to tell me how much she cared. She didn't talk to me at all. She'd tell me to go to my room, to entertain myself. She never showed much affection.

"And I think about my mom, and how she was raised. I don't know much, except that her father was really strict. He also didn't show her very much love. He wasn't taught how to do such a thing, and neither were his mother and father, when his grandparents were the children of people who were so afraid that their babies would be ripped away and sold, and so did not let themselves love the children they brought into this world. My goodness," my mom says, "I don't think I've ever let myself realize, until now, how much pain can be passed down. How much trauma can be inherited in every new generation. I regret the part I've played in that inheritance now."

There's something in the room—in the corner of my eye. I didn't notice it before. Maybe it wasn't there until this moment, or maybe it's been here all along. It's a dark haze, an unmoving figure. I see the Shadow, but I don't have any fear. I'm not afraid because I can see that it isn't the same one that has always followed. It isn't here for me.

This is a Shadow that belongs to my mother. It's her, the outline of what she might look like if she were an eclipse. This Shadow stares only at my mother, unblinkingly.

"It's been so long since I've thought about any of this," she says. "I told myself there wasn't any point to it, but was I wrong? Maybe there is a point to it all. Maybe it's actually the point of everything, to look at the things we'd rather look away from. The ways we're hurting, and the ways we've hurt other people, too. I think I might have hurt Moon. I never wanted to, but I did, just the same way my mother probably never wanted to hurt me, but she did, too."

My mom leans back in the seat and rests her eyes. "You're welcome to stay, little spirit child, but I won't be able to help you. That's the one thing I learned, long ago, from the time I first spoke to people who had passed on. There generally comes a time when you'll need to help yourself."

By the time I leave the apartment, my mother's fallen asleep in her seat.

I don't have to wonder where I need to go or what I need to do any longer. It feels like the tides of the sea guide me, and the answer comes, the answer that has been within me all along. The woods are darker beneath the ocean, with little light filtering through the leaves of trees. The clearing is in shadow—not because of the lack of light, but because of the being that waits for me.

The Shadow that has followed me, hunted me, chased me—always crying out, begging to finally meet me—stands patiently now. It's like it became more patient over time because it knew, somehow, that I was learning and growing and changing inside, and that soon I would stop hiding. That I would be the one to come and find them.

The haze grows from the Shadow like smoke from the tip of a flame, and darkness flickers and shudders even beneath the waves.

I land on my feet.

I face the Shadow, and the Shadow faces me.

I let myself look closely, for the first time in my life. And I see.

Yes, there's the truth: the truth I was so afraid to look at all along.

It's so clear now, that the Shadow is me.

They are another version of Moon, an outline against the light. The harder I stare, the more I can see the pain, the anguish in their face, the tears that haven't fallen yet.

This creature is not only me, but it's everything that I hate about myself. The more I have hated myself, the more the shadow and smoke have grown.

And I know what the answer has been all along, of course I do—it's the answer that is inside each and every one of us from the time we're born, from the time we enter this world.

I need to love myself.

Yes, even this part of me. Especially this part of me.

But it feels impossible, to do something like that.

How can I ever learn to love me? Even telling myself that I do only makes me feel ashamed, like I'm lying, and it isn't enough to say that I will learn to love myself eventually. I need to love myself, and my Shadow, right now.

I hold my breath, and I walk closer to the Shadow, who watches me with tears in their eyes. I swallow as I reach out a hand. The shadow child starts to cry—not the wailing sounds that have haunted me, but real tears that fall from their eyes. They've been so alone all this time, in so much pain, afraid I would never look at them, never find them, never want to see them. I look at them now, and I decide that I will try.

I think to myself that I love them.

The smoke around the child flickers.

I think it again, and again.

I love them.

I love them.

I love them.

I love this shadow.

And if I love them, then I love myself, too.

We're the same, aren't we?

I love me.

I love me.

I love me.

I think about the love I have for my mom. For Wolf and Dragon and the Magician, and I imagine loving myself with that same love, because I deserve it, too, in the same way that I love the earth beneath my feet and the trees that surround me and the sun and the moon.

The haze lightens. Golden light begins to fill the clearing.

I stand there for maybe a few minutes or a few hours or a few days, repeating the phrase, these words I never would have said a few months ago, these words that bite into me with shame as I feel the shadow inside me demand why it is that I deserve this love of mine. I ignore the voice, and I continue for so long that, after a while, the shame lightens; and after a while, a small part of me, for the length of a second or perhaps an eternity, feels how much I love myself right here and now—so completely, so fully, simply because I'm here. I exist.

I am worthy of love. I love myself, unconditionally, because I am a part of this universe.

I wrap my arms around the shadow of myself. "I love you, Moon."

My heart beats—a gentle thud—and I can feel the tides sucking away. Water lowers around me, drying into the ground. The Shadow slowly fades away. I can still feel them. I know that they're with me, inside me. They probably always will be. But this time, I know they're there. And I can remind myself, whenever I need to, that I love them, because I love myself.

CARNATION

I walk up the apartment steps. I'm completely dry, as if I'd never been beneath the ocean to begin with.

Maybe I wasn't. Maybe it was all in my head.

Maybe I was. Maybe I was drifting in yet another realm.

When I open the front door, the bells jingle. My mom's back is to me as she sits on the sofa. She turns around and her eyes widen.

"Moon?" she says, getting to her feet. She blinks, and I can tell that she's forgotten that she couldn't even remember me. "Where in the world have you been?"

She probably wouldn't want the real answer to that question. She probably wouldn't understand the spirit world or my Shadow or Wolf or Dragon or magicians.

I don't know how to explain everything that has happened, and nothing at all.

"I started to become sad again," I tell her, but even those words don't feel like they're enough. They don't explain everything I've been feeling. There aren't enough words in our language. "But I think I might start to feel happy soon, too."

I wipe my eyes, and she hurries to my side as I begin to cry. She kneels beside me. She looks at my face for so long that I wonder if she's trying to find the right words to say. She wraps her arms around me and pulls me in close.

"You're angry at me," I tell her.

She pulls back. "Why would I be mad at you, Moon?"

"Because I told you the truth. Because I said I'm depressed, and that sometimes I feel like I want to die, too."

My mom lets out a shaking breath. "I wasn't angry with you. I was scared. I was afraid. I'm still terrified, even now—terrified that I'm going to lose you."

I try to hear her words. She'd said something similar, too, when she didn't know that I was the spirit child she was talking to.

"I want to do what I can to help you, but I don't always know the answer." She takes a breath, unable to let it out again for a long moment. "I think that we adults," she starts, then stops, then tries again. "Sometimes we have to pretend to always know what to say. But we're human, and we make mistakes. If I ever did or said anything to make you think I was angry with you for feeling the way you do, then that was a mistake, and I'm so sorry. I was uncomfortable and didn't know what to say, but I can see how that's hurt you, and I'm sorry, Moon."

She hugs me again. "You're my universe."

And even though these words don't make everything better, I think I'm recognizing the beginnings of that feeling called hope.

SUMMER SNOWFLAKE

I've stopped disappearing. My hand is back, all its color and its skin. Joy had said a part of me didn't want to be in the world of the living, and even though sadness still moves through me like an old friend, I think I'm feeling changes. I might just want to be here, in the world of the living, more than I want to be in the realm of the spirits.

Andrew is back at school. Lilah and Wiley act like he'd never left. Andrew looks so bewildered that I know he must have been wandering, confused about why no one could see him, too. I wonder if that's why some people began to vanish. They were the ones who didn't want to be in the world of the living, either, even if no one else knew. I thought I was the only one. It doesn't make me glad that other people like Andrew have been just as sad as me all along—but I think it's good to know that I'm not alone anymore.

When our teacher tells us to work on a history assignment, Andrew looks up as we open our textbooks. "Um," he says suddenly. "Did anything . . . weird happen?" he asks.

Lilah and Wiley look at each other. "Weird how?" Lilah asks.

"Like . . . Did I . . . I don't know . . . stop coming to class one day?"

Wiley frowns. "No. You were here every day, with us. Don't you remember?"

Andrew looks frustrated. He shakes his head. "Never mind."

Lilah and Wiley both shrug as they go back to doing their work. Andrew looks up at me just as I realize I'm staring at him. Even though my heart patters with fear, I offer him a smile. He hesitates, then gives a soft smile back.

When school is over, I'm surprised by a tap on my shoulder. Andrew follows me out of the pod, his mask on. "Hey," he says, "can I talk to you for a second? Maybe I'm just making things up in my head, but I felt like you knew what I was talking about earlier when I asked if I'd been at class, and . . ." He stops, watching me with hope.

Should I tell him the truth? I don't think anyone in the world of the living would believe my story. Maybe he'll only laugh at me or make fun of me. But I want to believe that not everyone in this world wants to hurt me. I want to trust that I could talk to someone, and that they might even grow to like me and my wings.

"Yes," I tell Andrew. "I knew. And . . . well, I kind of disappeared at one point, too."

Andrew looks relieved. "I knew I wasn't crazy!"

I laugh a little. Andrew's outburst reminds me of Dragon. Dragon, who I left behind with Wolf and the Monster. The Monster, who I have to face tonight. I try to keep the quiver of fear out of my voice. This is the most I've spoken in the world of the living in a while now, but I want to keep talking.

"What *is* crazy, anyway?" I ask him.

He shrugs. "I don't know. Anything different, I guess. That's what my old podmates called me all the time. They said I'm crazy for believing in weird things like spirits and aliens."

My smile swells. "Maybe people are called crazy like it's a bad thing so that we'll want to be just like everyone else. So we stop thinking about how different things could be instead. I bet a lot of people who changed the world because they thought differently from everyone else were once called crazy also."

Andrew seems thoughtful. "Your definition of crazy doesn't sound too bad," he says.

"I think I want to be called crazy now."

"Yeah. Me, too."

We laugh and grin at each other, even behind our masks.

Wolf always told me I haven't had a chance to meet my friends yet. Maybe he was onto something.

Andrew and I walk down the block, and we talk about how we both disappeared, and Andrew gives me his theories on what it all meant and what actually happened, and that we were really taken away by aliens and had new memories implanted, and I think I'm just a little happier, being here, in the world of the living, and being weird with him.

★

My mom and I spend time together after school. She doesn't expect me to speak, so some moments there's nothing but silence, and in that silence I get to know her, and she gets to know me. She watches shows with me on the boxy TV, and I tell her about Andrew and Lilah and Wiley. My mom opens the photo album that she keeps on the living room floor, and sits with me as I slip through the pages, looking at the pictures. I see her as a little girl, and I see her father, who I've never met, not here or in the spirit world.

I pause when I see a picture of her standing beside an older woman. The woman has dark gray hair and an unsmiling face. She looks so stern. I'd be afraid to stand next to her. I know who she is immediately. I've seen her so many afternoons now. It's only as I'm looking at them side by side in the photo that I see all the similarities. The same nose and same eyes. I'm not even as surprised as I probably should be. Maybe a part of me already knew who she was all along.

"That's my mother," my mom says, pressing a corner of the photo with her fingertip, gently, like she's afraid to touch it. "We didn't have the best relationship when I was younger. I promised myself, when I had you, that things would be different." She doesn't say the words, but I can feel the disappointment in her—that, maybe, she thinks she hasn't changed as much as she'd wished.

"Things are different," I say.

Her smile crinkles her eyes and she puts a hand on mine, the same hand that had been disappearing all this time. The person my mom has been looking after for so many weeks has now passed away. They've gone to the spirit realm, where they're probably lost, wandering, unsure of where to go, now that the Keeper has turned into the Monster. I don't know. Maybe they've entered an entirely different realm. My mom doesn't have a new person to take care of yet, but she's tired and decides to go to bed early. She kisses my forehead and lets her hand linger on my cheek before she leaves, reminding me not to stay up too late.

I sit on the sofa, waiting. The front door opens and closes, and Ms. Stella walks into the living room. She isn't the same young woman as before, when she would visit me every evening. She isn't the age of my mom, the same age as when she had my mother, the same age as when my mother had me. She's just as old as she was in the photograph, but that stern, grim expression is gone. She has a smile for me as she lets out a gentle breath of relief and sits in the same place she always does.

"Why didn't you say?" I ask her.

"There are some secrets that are better kept hidden," she says. "This wasn't about me, and who I am. This has always been about you, Moon."

"What has been about me? Why are you here?" I pause, and realization floods through me. "You're my guardian."

"The third and final that you needed to find. And now you've found me. Isn't that wonderful?"

"I thought that all guardians were in the higher realms."

"Not all of us," my grandmother says. "Sometimes we're ancestors. I was glad to volunteer to be your guardian, Moon."

"Did you always know I would need you?"

"Time is different in the spirit realms. The time you have in your mind now is an illusion, too. Doesn't that mean, then, that while you sit here before me, there's also a Moon that exists from before you were even born? There's an older Moon, too, who has always looked out for you. And there's also a Moon who knows the answer you seek already. You know what it is you need. You have always known."

I think I do know the answer. I know how to

defeat the Monster. "But I'm afraid."

"Yes," my grandmother says. "Change is scary, isn't it? It can be terrifying to turn to new ways. That's why adults struggle so much with change, I think," she says. "So set in the old ways. We don't even want to consider change sometimes."

"I want to," I say. "I hope the whole world changes."

"Children, children, golden children," she says. "A new era is coming because of you."

When I blink and breathe, my grandmother doesn't sit across from me in the living room anymore.

I almost stand out of my seat.

She wouldn't leave just like that, would she?

She can't have gone without saying goodbye to me.

But even as I think this, there's an answer in my head. My grandmother was watching over me long before she walked into this apartment building. She's still watching me, even now—still helping me, guiding me, just like Joy and Wisdom, and many other guardians I haven't even met. I know what she wants. All she's ever wanted, my grandmother, is for me to be happy. To know that I'm loved.

And yes. I do know the answer, after all.

BLUESTAR

The spirit world has a purple sky and dark clouds that spin, tornadoes racing across the ground in the distance. Vines and thorns have taken over the land so much that I have to watch every step. As I walk closer, the howls and cries find me, and crowds of Shadows begin to gather, walking closer, watching me with hollow eyes. Whose Shadows are these? Are they the Shadows of all the beings who are asleep? Wolf is buried, just like every other being, beneath the vines and thorns. I can't even see him. I can't even touch him. I swallow, straighten my back, and I walk past the line of Shadows, not stopping as I reach the pyramid's doors.

I step into the marble corridor. Roots cover the walls completely now. The lights blink and flicker on. I walk down one hall and another, remembering the maze, until one door slides up. Even the world surrounding the old manor is shrouded in clouds, covering the blue sky and its sun. The garden is dead, the manor's walls crumbling.

And there, standing in front of the house, is the Monster.

"Keeper," I say. "I'm here to free Wolf and Dragon, and all the beings who are trapped here because of you."

The Keeper doesn't have any resemblance to the woman I first met. She's morphed into a being with chalky white skin, and she's so tall that her neck stretches to the top of the manor. I have to stare up at her. I can tell that her eyes, even from so high, are just as pale and unblinking as ever.

This is the body she has transformed into.

But she wasn't always like this.

I wonder who she was before she was this being, which I'd called the Monster. I wonder who she was before the Keeper, too.

I wonder who she was when she was a child, looking for love, just like I was.

"You are so brave," the Keeper says, her voice echoing from above. "Why else would you return here, knowing that you will never leave again?"

Her words are meant to scare me, to make me feel like I am less than her.

I stand taller. "I'm here to free Wolf and Dragon," I say again, "and all the beings who are trapped here because of you."

"Free Wolf and Dragon," she scoffs, then laughs, her voice echoing. "And what about yourself?" the Keeper asks me. Even from so far above, I can hear her sneer. "Do you believe you can save yourself? You have already vanished once in the world of the living. You fade in and out because a part of you still wants to remain here. And perhaps you should," she says. "The world of the living is filled with so much pain and suffering. There are so many who do not love you. There are so many who want to hurt you. Do you want to know what's even worse?" she asks. "You know that you deserve that pain."

"You're wrong."

"You know that you don't deserve anyone's love. It's why you hate yourself so much."

"I do deserve love," I tell her. "I deserve love from others and from myself. Every being is made of love. I am, too. I love myself," I say. Hasn't this been the answer, all along? "I've needed to learn how. It won't always be easy to do. And sometimes I will forget—but right here, right now, I love myself. Do you?"

The Keeper stills. Her head swivels and drives down to meet me, hair rising all around her. "What a ridiculous question! Yes, of course I love myself. I love myself more than you and anyone else. I deserve more love than you. I'm more powerful than all of you."

I tilt my head back to look at her. It becomes more and more clear, the longer she is in front of me. How much pain she really is in. "Are you sure?" I ask.

She screeches with rage. "Yes, you brat, I'm sure!"

"If you love yourself," I tell her, "then wouldn't you understand that everyone is worthy of the same love, too?"

"You've been talking to your guardians, I see," she says. "You think you're so wise. My guardian comes here to me also, but all they ever say are lies."

I wonder who the Keeper was when she was a child. I think she might have been a little more like me than I realize. "You take the love of others, the light and lives of souls, because you hate your own."

She narrows her eyes to dangerous slits. "And you

sound just like them," she says. "You're speaking lies, too. You're liars. All of you."

I want to know who hurt her, who made her feel like she was alone, who told her the lie that she didn't deserve love. "Why do you hate yourself so much?" I ask her. "Why don't you believe that you deserve love, too?"

She releases a scream that forces me to clamp my hands over my ears. She stands tall again, neck stretching, her head peering down at me. "Love? What is the point of it all when you will only die anyway, and you will come back here, to the spirit realm? Everyone around me returns to the stars, given a chance to return to that unending source of power. But not me. Never me."

I didn't think I would ever feel bad for the Keeper, but I do.

I feel bad for her because I know who she is now.

I shake my head. "That's not true. You haven't been able to rise because you never learned to feel love for yourself. You stayed here in the spirit realm, and you've hated yourself all this time. I'm sorry. No one deserves to feel that pain."

But my words only bring Blue more rage. She grows in size before my eyes. Fire burns from the corners of her mouth and in her nostrils.

"It's because you were in pain," I tell her. "It's because you were in pain that you hurt so many. It's why you need to see so many others in pain, too."

"I'm not in pain," Blue screams. Even though she has taken this form, I know she is still the child she'd once been. She's been a child, like me, all this time. My imagination pulled from the spirit world, and I learned her story: a girl who died too young and learned the wrong meaning of power.

"You don't know me," she says. "You don't know anything about me. You're the one who is angry. It isn't my fault that there isn't a point to anything, to any of this. There's no point to life when you're going to die in the end."

"The point," I say, "is that I am still alive. There will be hurt. I will be sad. But I know I'll be happy, too. And I will learn and grow from the mistakes I make. I know that I'll meet people who will love me for who I am. I already have, and there will be more. The point is that I'll get to experience joy and laughter. The world of the living is an adventure, and I'm excited to discover it. I'm excited to live."

"You're lying to yourself."

"And I forgive you," I tell her.

Blue jerks back. "What?"

"I forgive you for everything. It's what you deserve, too. We all make mistakes."

She shrinks away, like she isn't sure what to say.

"Sometimes those mistakes are horrible. But that's not who we really are, right?" I ask her. "Those mistakes were made by people who were hurting and afraid."

"I didn't make any mistakes!"

"We call each other monsters because we don't want to look at the ways we've hurt others. And we have to fix our mistakes when we can."

"You don't know what you're talking about!"

"But underneath that fear and anger and pain, we're all really made of love."

"What're you doing?" she demands. "Stop!"

"You're made of love, too," I remind her. "So, if everyone is made of love, then that means we all love each other, even if we don't realize it."

"Why're you saying this?" she cries.

"Everyone in the world and every being in every realm already loves each other, without even knowing each other. That means I love you, too, Blue."

She lurches. A light escapes her mouth, a silvery blue firefly glowing in the air, twinkling before it disappears. Her eyes widen. She hiccups, and more blue lights float from her mouth. Another, and another—the air is filled with balls of light now, floating from her mouth and her skin. Blue becomes smaller and smaller as the lights fade away.

"People will try to convince me otherwise," I say, "but my life is worth living. I deserve to exist as much as anyone else. I'm happy I'm still alive, and that there's so much I will get to experience."

Blue is a woman again, the same I'd first met, and even then she grows smaller. Another light, and another—and one that slowly appears from her chest.

And in front of me is only the child. The same one who has come to me in my dreams, the same one who fills my imagination and my stories. Blue is crying. Her face shines wet as she stands in front of me. I wonder when she'd last been in this form, or if this is who she'd been all along. This child, crying, who needed so much love.

There's a hollow sound. It vibrates through the air. It's the familiar wailing, the longing of a Shadow. It's time. She has to face what she hasn't wanted to look at for the past hundreds of thousands of years, in both the world of the living and in the spirit realm. This is something I already know I can't help her with.

I turn to leave but pause, surprised when I hear Blue call my name.

"Please," she says. "Don't leave me with it. Don't leave me alone."

I know the feeling of being afraid of the Shadow. I also ran away from it for so long.

It was always so terrifying, wasn't it?

To have to face all that pain.

"But if you meet your Shadow," I say, "then you can begin to grow."

CHRYSANTHEMUM

Outside the pyramid, the thorns and vines that twisted through the city melt away, shedding layers of flower petals so much it's a miracle I'm not having a sneezing fit. The sky has gone from darkness to radiant swirling colors, almost like it's having a celebration of bright fireworks. I see blobs of lights, pink and yellow and silver and gold, flying across the top of the realm—guardians, who have come to cheer.

The beings are cheering, too. They're waking up, standing from the ground, some mumbling in confusion while others clap and laugh, hugging one another.

Dragon is waiting for me outside the pyramid. They leap into the air with a whoop and run up to me, grasping my hands to spin me around, joy shining on their face and in their scales. "You did it, Moon!" they say.

I laugh, a bubble of joy rising in me, too.

I'm happy, happier than I've been in so long, so happy that I start to cry.

But the bubble deflates. My smile falls, and Dragon's smile becomes sadder now also. I know that this moment will one day be a long-ago memory. I know I'll never see Dragon again—and from the look in their eyes, they know this as well.

"The sky hasn't been this bright in . . ." They pause to count on their fingers. "Over twenty thousand years," they say, grin growing. "Thanks to you, things around here are going to be different."

"I wish you could come with me," I say. It isn't fair. Dragon wants to be alive so badly.

"Me, too," they say. "But you . . . There's so much still waiting for you. I won't be by your side, not any-more, but I will always be your friend here in the spirit world. And who knows. Maybe, someday soon, I'll man-age to make my way over again, too."

I hug Dragon. "Thank you for helping me."

They smile into the hug. "You're welcome, Moon."

"What will you do now?"

They sigh and look up to the sky. "I don't know.

Seeing you have the courage to face the Keeper and go back to the world of the living makes me think that maybe it's time. Maybe I should go to the higher realms."

I giggle a little. It's hard to imagine Dragon as an old, wise guardian. They meet my eye and snort, probably laughing at the same exact thing. "If I play my cards right and prank a few guardians, they might just kick me out again. Maybe they'll even give me a chance to live another life. Maybe I'll meet you," they tell me, "in a completely different body, and I won't even recognize you, but you'll think I seem familiar, and before you know it, we'll be friends."

"I would like that a lot, Dragon."

We stand together in a shared silence.

"It hurts, but we have to say goodbye now," they say, sounding older and wiser, and I actually think that maybe they could do really well as a guardian. "But I'll always be with you. I'm always watching over you from the spirit realm. Will you remember that, Moon?"

"I will. I'll remember you for the rest of my life, and even after that."

They let go of my hands.

I know I have to leave.

I also know that I'm excited for the life that's waiting for me.

But what comes next. That's what I'm dreading the most.

I'm dreading the next few moments, more than anything.

The tears have already filled me by the time I reach the trees at the edge of the city. I walk through the bark, through the grass and fallen branches, until I reach a clearing.

Wolf sits patiently, watching me, waiting for me, like he has always done—a hundred times, and a thousand times, always ready for me to come. He'd been my only friend for so long. A part of me is afraid I'll never meet another friend like him again. That I'll never meet someone that I've loved as much as him. But isn't that the adventure of life? The wondering what might just happen next.

I run to Wolf and hug as much of him as I can, burying myself in his fur.

Well done, little Moon, he says.

I don't want this to be the end. I don't want to leave

him. "I've missed you so much. I was afraid I'd never see you awake again."

I know. I'm sorry I wasn't there to help you. But I watched over you, always, even then. You amazed me, Moon. You faced your fears and your Shadow. You showed love to yourself and to Blue. I'm so proud of you.

And now, just as I've gotten him back, I have to say goodbye. I know I can't come back to the spirit realm. I'll never see him again.

It isn't the end, he lets me know. *There is no such thing as an end in this universe. There are only new beginnings, again and again, moving from one volume in your life so that you can open the next. I love you, Moon. As you grow, and you become an adult, and you begin to wonder if your journeys here to this realm were real or not, that is the one thing I hope you will always remember: I love you so, so much. I will always be with you, even in the world of the living. If you ever see the image of a wolf or my name written in a story, know that it is me. It's a sign that I am with you—protecting you and watching over you, as always. Do you believe this?*

I nod against his fur, gasping through the tears.

Oh, little Moon. I know that you are sad. I am, too. He rests his head on my shoulder and releases a slow breath.

I'm afraid to ask my next question. "Will I ever see you again?"

Yes, Wolf says, *in another lifetime. I will always be here. I'll always be waiting. But there's a life that's waiting for you first, my dear, sweet child. Live.*

It's time.

MOONFLOWER

I'm so glad that I'm still alive.

There's still sadness. There are still times when I cry myself to sleep at night.

But there's laughter, too. I laugh with Andrew and Lilah and Wiley. I laugh with my mom as we watch TV. I wonder about the future, and everything that's waiting for me. The friends I haven't met yet and the people who don't even know me but love me already.

I spend time writing my stories.

I wonder how much this world might change.

The world you and I both share.

My world, the world of the living.

The tree inside me is starting to blossom now, I think.

A NOTE
FROM THE AUTHOR

When I was a child, I would often sit in the woods outside of my school and close my eyes and try to leave my body so that I could fly away, never coming back again. I was diagnosed with depression, and like the main character of this novel, Moon, I would cry myself to sleep almost every night, praying that I wouldn't wake up in the morning, always disappointed when I did.

My depression has stayed with me my entire life. Though traditional treatments have been lifesaving for many, medication and therapy never helped me and, in some cases, made my depression and suicidal ideation worse. It was only until I was thirty years old that my internal world shifted.

I began to remember that I have a unique purpose in this world, as does every human being. I saw that those who have hurt us, both intentionally and unintentionally, have also been hurt, and that my forgiveness and compassion granted me release. I realized that we are not alone in this vast universe of energy, and that each and every one of us is so unconditionally adored. I learned, above all else, that I am worthy of existence and love.

These were some of the lessons that helped me find excitement and joy for my life in the world of the living —lessons that I wanted to share through Moon as they learn these lessons, too. While depression can't be cured, I hope that Moon's journey may resonate for some as I gift this story to my younger self, and that, above all else, readers will feel that they are worthy of unconditional love and acceptance.

Here are some helpful resources.

National Suicide Prevention Lifeline: 800-273-8255 for chat, and for text line, text HOME to 741741 to reach a crisis counselor.

The suicide prevention lifeline website: https://suicidepreventionlifeline.org/help-yourself/youth/.

ACKNOWLEDGMENTS

Thank you to Beth Phelan, who really went above and beyond as an agent, and Gallt & Zacker Literary.

Thank you to Andrea Davis Pinkney, Jennifer Thompson, David Levithan, Emily Heddleson, Taylan Salvati, Lizette Serrano, Michael Strouse, Lauren Donovan, Matt Poulter, Deimosa Webber-Bey, and the rest of the Scholastic team. Thank you to Daniel Minter for bringing the cover of *Moonflower* to life.

A huge thank-you to Tehlor Kay Mejia and Ashley Herring Blake for reading *Moonflower* and giving me the clarity I needed.

Thank you also to Pamela Hoffman, MD, Medical Director for Telehealth Services for Yale New Haven Health System and Yale Medicine, and Assistant Professor, Child Psychiatry, Yale Child Study Center, for reading and sharing your thoughts.

And, finally, thank you to the readers whose support and love of stories inspires me.

ABOUT THE AUTHOR

Kacen Callender is the bestselling and award-winning author of multiple novels for children, teens, and adults, including the National Book Award–winning and Coretta Scott King Author Honor–winning *King and the Dragonflies*, which also won the Lambda Literary Award; *Hurricane Child*, winner of the Stonewall Book Award and the Lambda Literary Award; and the bestselling novel *Felix Ever After*. Kacen enjoys playing RPG video games, practicing their art, and focusing on healing and growth in their free time. They currently reside in St. Thomas of the US Virgin Islands, where they were born and raised.